Chris...

Two hospita...

Great Sout... ...spital in London and
Great Northern Hospital in Edinburgh are very special
places. Their close working relationship allows them
to share their considerable talents and world-class
knowledge, from transplant and reconstructive
surgery to neurosurgery and cutting-edge cancer
research. As the festive season begins, and the
sparkle of fairy lights fills the hospital gardens,
staff will be saving lives—and falling in love!

Immerse yourself in the warmth and romance
of the season with...

Tamsin and Max's story
Festive Fling with the Surgeon by Karin Baine

Lauren and Oliver's story
A Mistletoe Marriage Reunion by Louisa Heaton

Skye and Jay's story
Melting Dr. Grumpy's Frozen Heart by Scarlet Wilson

Poppy and Dylan's story
Neurosurgeon's IVF Mix-Up Miracle by Annie Claydon

All available now!

Dear Reader,

Sometimes a book just "clicks" with me. Take two people who've both had a lot to deal with but who reckon they have their lives sorted now, add one mistake and suddenly they both have an overarching reason to negotiate everything that they've previously taken for granted...

Poppy and Dylan were those people, and it was pure pleasure to write their story. The baby they've made together is a blessing, but they're going to have to work hard to allow each other to give their child the best of both of them.

As I wrote, Dylan and Poppy just jumped off the page toward me. Thank you for reading their story, and I hope you enjoy it as much as I did!

Annie x

NEUROSURGEON'S IVF MIX-UP MIRACLE

ANNIE CLAYDON

MEDICAL ROMANCE

Special thanks and acknowledgment are given to Annie Claydon for her contribution to the Christmas North and South miniseries.

Harlequin®
MEDICAL
ROMANCE

Recycling programs
for this product may
not exist in your area.

ISBN-13: 978-1-335-94269-2

Neurosurgeon's IVF Mix-Up Miracle

Copyright © 2024 by Harlequin Enterprises ULC

For questions and comments about the quality of this book, please contact us at CustomerService@Harlequin.com.

Harlequin Enterprises ULC
22 Adelaide St. West, 41st Floor
Toronto, Ontario M5H 4E3, Canada
www.Harlequin.com

Printed in U.S.A.

Cursed with a poor sense of direction and a propensity to read, **Annie Claydon** spent much of her childhood lost in books. A degree in English literature followed by a career in computing didn't lead directly to her perfect job—writing romance for Harlequin—but she has no regrets in taking the scenic route. She lives in London, a city where getting lost can be a joy.

Books by Annie Claydon

Harlequin Medical Romance

The Best Man and the Bridesmaid
Greek Island Fling to Forever
Falling for the Brooding Doc
The Doctor's Reunion to Remember
Risking It All for a Second Chance
From the Night Shift to Forever
Stranded with the Island Doctor
Snowbound by Her Off-Limits GP
Cinderella in the Surgeon's Castle
Children's Doc to Heal Her Heart
One Summer in Sydney
Healed by Her Rival Doc
Country Fling with the City Surgeon
Winning Over the Off-Limits Doctor

Visit the Author Profile page
at Harlequin.com for more titles.

CHAPTER ONE

MONDAY LUNCHTIME. Eight months pregnant and summoned to the fertility clinic by a telephone call from her doctor that morning. Just for a *little chat* to tie up some loose ends. If she could come at lunchtime, that would be perfect. Would half past twelve suit her?

Poppy Evans wasn't entirely buying it. Dr Patel had sounded positive and upbeat, but had also insisted firmly that their meeting couldn't wait until later in the week. In her experience, that kind of invitation wasn't usually issued for loose ends of no consequence, and Poppy had spent the short taxi ride from the Great Southern Hospital to the fertility clinic trying not to list out possibilities in her head.

She was keeping it all under control. After all, she was a neurosurgeon—the kind of person who always had a steady hand and a cool head, whatever the situation. But as she approached the young woman behind the reception desk she felt her heart lurch with anxiety.

'Poppy Evans for Dr Patel.'

The receptionist smiled, turning to a computer screen. 'Thank you, I'll let her know you're here. Would you like to take a seat in the waiting room?'

Poppy remembered to return the smile, before walking through to the large, sensitively organised space. Groups of seats were organised around small occasional tables, with green plants and low-level partitions giving some semblance of privacy. No one needed to meet anyone else's gaze if they didn't want to, and Poppy had appreciated that when she'd first visited the clinic. She'd been able to pretend that the pregnant women, waiting with their partners, didn't have everything that she'd once wanted.

If only Nate were here now…

Nate would understand how she felt. He'd listen to every one of her fears and wouldn't try to dismiss them or tell her not to worry. He'd simply take her hand between his and tell her that he'd always be there for her, and that whatever came next they'd get through it together.

But Nate wasn't here. When they'd made their vows and promised to love each other for the rest of their lives, neither of them could possibly have foreseen that Nate's heart was a ticking time bomb. They'd been together for seven years and married for barely three on that fateful winter's morning when Poppy had stood on the touch-line, cheering the Great Southern team on in an inter-hospital football match. Nate had been the goalie for the team and just before half-time he'd made a dive for the ball. His heart had stopped before he hit the ground, and despite heroic efforts by his teammates he'd been beyond saving.

Poppy had spent every waking moment aching with grief. Every sleeping moment dreaming of the love she'd lost. The children that she and Nate had wanted together, deciding to wait for a few years after their wedding because they had all the time in the world…

Then Nate had come to her rescue. He would never have expected her to live her life alone, and although Poppy couldn't bear to love anyone else the way she'd loved him she had plenty of room in her heart for a child. She'd taken her time to grieve, then gone through counselling and made new promises for the future, which had brought her here.

'Hey there, baby…' Poppy shifted uncomfortably in her seat, trying to find that elusive position of perfect relaxation, her mouth forming the shape of the words. *'It's going to be all right. You and I, we're in this together.'*

Somehow, that gave her the answer she needed. Poppy took a breath and then another, as instinct and unquestioning love began to steady her nerves.

'Dylan Harper. I'm a little early.' A voice that she knew floated over from the reception desk and Poppy looked up. The man was facing the receptionist, but one glance at the shock of blond hair and the perfectly fitting grey suit was enough to tell Poppy that she hadn't misheard. However unlikely, this was the Dylan Harper she knew.

Not well—although she and Dylan were both neurosurgeons at the Great Southern Hospital, he had a busy schedule. It wasn't easy to combine his role of hotshot surgeon, a man who could take on the most difficult cases and achieve the best possible result, with all of that gorgeous charm and sex appeal, which he shared liberally with a string of different partners. Their paths had inevitably crossed, and she'd been impressed with his skill and professionalism, but she'd left it at that. His deep blue eyes didn't have the same power over Poppy as they seemed to wield over practically every other female member of the department.

Forget it. She had her own concerns and now wasn't the time to wonder what business Dylan might have at a fertility clinic. Poppy rolled her eyes, annoyed with herself for wondering what Dylan was up to when it really wasn't any of her business, and with him for... She wasn't quite sure what Dylan had done to annoy her. A multitude of small niggles that boiled down to the fact that he didn't appear to value the things that she did.

The receptionist was waving him straight through to the corridor behind her, where the consulting rooms were located. Apparently, he wasn't going to be asked to wait, even though he was early. Poppy shifted again in her seat and saw Dr Patel hurrying towards her.

'Hi, Poppy.' Something about her smile lacked its usual warmth. Perhaps she was just having a bad day. 'How are you?'

'I was thinking that you might tell *me*.' Poppy was getting a little frustrated, and wished that someone would get to the point and tell her why she was here.

'Yes…yes, of course. This isn't a medical matter…we just need to have a chat.'

Enough with the code words and vague reassurances. 'My baby's all right?' This wasn't really the place to ask, but the waiting room was empty and it was the only question that Poppy needed to know the answer to.

Dr Patel suddenly looked her straight in the eye. That was better. 'I've reviewed all your notes and your baby's fine. Come with me, and we'll talk.'

Okay. Dylan had disappeared now and Poppy

followed Dr Patel to her consulting room. She refused the offer of a cup of herbal tea, and was waved over to an informal seating area to one side of the desk.

Dr Patel sat down opposite her. 'As you know, Poppy, we have very strict procedures to ensure that the rights and confidentiality of both our donors and recipients are protected.'

Poppy nodded. That was exactly what she'd wanted. This baby was the one that she'd longed for, and which she and Nate couldn't have. The list of traits which had helped her to choose a father for her child had been all the better for being impersonal.

'I can only apologise for this—'

'Get to the point!' Poppy regretted the words immediately and shot Dr Patel an apologetic look. 'Please. I've always appreciated your straightforwardness, and that's what I need from you now.'

Dr Patel nodded, concern flashing in her eyes. 'I have to tell you that the biological father of the child you're carrying is not the donor that you chose.'

What? Poppy pressed her lips together, aware that she should probably keep her first thoughts to herself, and give the information a chance to sink in. Dr Patel was watching her, a concerned look on her face, and thankfully giving her time to process it all.

'You mean…?' Poppy still couldn't think of a coherent question. 'Say that again…'

Dr Patel nodded, swallowing hard. 'A mistake was made at the facility we use to store donations, and your eggs were fertilised with sperm from the wrong donor.'

Okay. That didn't leave any room for doubt. Poppy took a breath. 'How on earth did this happen?'

'As you know, we use an independent storage facility.' Dr Patel repeated the information a second time, in case Poppy had missed it the first. 'They informed us as soon as they were aware, and have cooperated with our request to give us access to their records. All of my enquiries over the weekend have convinced me that this is a genuine mistake.'

Poppy waved her hand abruptly and Dr Patel fell silent. 'When did you know about this? My baby hasn't been DNA tested—what makes you so sure that there even *has* been a mistake?'

'The facility called and spoke to me late on Friday afternoon. I spent most of Saturday there, going through their procedures, so that I would have a clear report to give to you today. There's a complete audit trail, backed up by hard copy records, which confirms exactly who the biological father of your baby is.'

'And it's not the person I chose.'

'No, it isn't.'

So there was no doubt. Poppy was about to have a child and had no idea who the father might be. The baby inside her seemed to pick up on her agitation and started to kick. She absent-mindedly rubbed her stomach to soothe it, and realised that she wasn't thinking straight. This was *her* baby. She'd carried it for eight months, looking after it for every step of the way. Nothing could make her love it any less, and it wasn't humanly possible to love it any more.

'So... If the records are so unequivocal, how did this happen?'

'The storage facility and this clinic have agreed on a joint enquiry, and I've been nominated to lead it. We're committed to maintaining transparency and keeping you informed.'

Right. Poppy wasn't used to being on this side of the conversation. She'd feel a lot happier if she was in control—making enquiries and drawing conclusions herself. She might have to fight those battles later, though, because she had a more pressing question.

'And the biological father of my baby...?'

'He was contacted yesterday and Dr Neave, the director of this clinic, spoke with him. He agreed immediately that you should have sight of his medical records, and also suggested that if you would like to meet with him he would be prepared to waive his own confidentiality rights.'

Another person who'd been told before she had. But it put Poppy in charge of at least part of the process, so she'd let that slide for the moment. The biological father probably wouldn't have the same medical understanding she had, but his gesture meant that she could ask him all the right questions, and hear his answers first-hand.

'Okay. I don't *want* to meet with him, but I think I need to. I'd be grateful if you would arrange that as soon as possible.'

'We can arrange it for you now. He's agreed to make himself available and is in this building, with Dr Neave. Or you can think about it— maybe sleep on it?' Dr Patel hesitated. 'Whatever you decide, I want you to know that I'll be with you all the way.'

There was nothing *to* decide. Poppy shook her head. 'You understand that I'm well equipped to make the best medical decisions for my child.'

Dr Patel smiled suddenly. 'Yes, I do.' She got to her feet, walking over to her desk to pick up a folder, which she handed to Poppy. 'For our own records, we need you to sign a waiver first, with regard to your own confidentiality rights.'

'You have a pen?' Poppy scanned the three copies of the document inside.

'Yes, I do. But you're going to take your time

and read everything through first. And I'm going to fetch you a cup of herbal tea, whether you want it or not.' Dr Patel's practical, dry humour surfaced and Poppy smiled.

'Yes, okay. Thanks. On second thoughts, I think I could do with a drink.'

Dylan Harper had thought about little else since yesterday afternoon. It had come as a shock to find that his sperm donation, which had been frozen some years previously, had been given to someone by mistake. A process that was shrouded in confidentiality suddenly seemed intensely personal.

He couldn't allow himself to have feelings, though. When the director of the fertility clinic had called him, Dylan had insisted on meeting with him straight away. Dr Neave had explained all his options and Dylan had made a decision. The anonymous woman who was carrying his baby was clearly the most vulnerable person in all of this and, as such, her needs and decisions should take priority over his. He'd waived his own confidentiality rights, and made himself available today.

The needs of the expectant mother—who Dylan was struggling not to think of as the mother of his baby—clearly didn't involve him at the moment. He'd been sitting in Dr Neave's office, waiting, for more than half an hour. Dr Neave had tried to engage him in conversation for a while and when that hadn't worked for either of them he'd left Dylan alone to read a magazine.

Maybe this had been a wasted journey. Dylan stared at the clock, wondering if he should leave, and then decided that he shouldn't because, however this turned out, the journey hadn't been wasted at all. It was all about options—and if the expectant mother rejected the option of meeting with him today, that was fine.

He sighed, leaning back in his seat and staring at the ceiling. Then jumped as Dr Neave came back into the office.

'The mother would like to meet you. Are you ready?' Dr Neave had already expressed his reservations about Dylan's insistence that she should take priority in everything, and told him that he was here to advocate for him.

'Far from it.' Dylan ignored Dr Neave's suggestion that he was perfectly within his rights to wait a while. 'Let's go, shall we?' He wasn't in the habit of going back on his decisions once they were made.

It took a slightly irritable hurry-up glare before Dr Neave joined him in the corridor, heading for one of the consulting rooms at the far end of the corridor. Dr Neave tapped on the door, waiting for a moment until a woman's voice sounded, inviting them in, and Dylan was ushered into the room.

Then the thunderbolt hit.

Two women were sitting on the sofa. The one who clearly *wasn't* pregnant would be Dr Patel, the deputy director of the clinic. And the one who very obviously was...

'Ms Evans.' The sudden, enforced intimacy of the situation felt as if it were strangling him and Dylan instinctively tried to draw back from the sensation. But even though they didn't know each other well, he and Poppy had never gone quite as far as referring to each other as Ms Evans and Mr Harper. 'Poppy...'

That might have been a wrong move. Poppy's eyes filled with tears and Drs Neave and Patel were looking at each other, seemingly at a loss. No surgeon liked to be wrong-footed, least of all Dylan Harper, but he knew exactly what he needed to do. Poppy's care was the one and only priority.

That wasn't going to be as easy as he'd imagined it might be. Dylan had always liked Poppy and moreover he respected her. She was the best surgeon in the whole department, with the possible exception of himself, and her intelligent, no-nonsense approach would beguile any man.

And she was beautiful, too. When she'd first

come to work at the Great Southern Hospital he'd regarded Poppy as gorgeous but strictly off-limits, because she was married. Then, when she'd lost her husband so tragically, Dylan had kept his distance even more assiduously, a little ashamed that Poppy's slim figure, red hair and expressive hazel eyes should still provoke a reaction in him.

And now she was in the full bloom of pregnancy, which seemed to push all of his buttons as well. Poppy had always been professional in their dealings, but if Dylan had to take a guess at her opinion of him he'd probably settle for mild dislike. Which didn't make him much of a candidate as biological father of her unborn child.

Of course, she'd never wanted a father for her child. She'd wanted an anonymous donor, who had passed all of the genetic screening and health tests. Even this much contact was more than she'd ever envisaged, and the fact that they knew each other made everything even worse.

One tear rolled down her cheek in the silence. Maybe he should say something, but for the life of him he couldn't think of anything that might be either helpful or appropriate. Telling her that surely it wasn't so bad to find that he was the biological father of her child felt more like a salve for his own ego than a reassurance.

'You're not operating today?' Poppy's voice quivered a little.

Fair enough. If she wanted to ignore the elephant in the room and discuss his operating schedule, then that might give them both a chance to get their breath back.

'No. I had two early morning procedures, and I may need to see a patient late this afternoon. Dr Shah will fill in for me if necessary.'

Poppy nodded. 'I was in post-op this morning. Both your patients are doing well.'

'That's good to hear. Thank you.' Dylan resisted the temptation to ask for a more detailed update. Right now, he could hardly remember what he'd been doing in the operating room this morning, which was unusual as he could usually give a blow-by-blow account of every procedure he'd performed at the end of each day.

He reminded himself that he'd decided to take on the role of protector, even if that had never been an option for either of them before. He walked forward, sitting down in the armchair opposite Poppy.

'This is a shock for both of us.' He took a breath, letting go of everything that his suddenly vulnerable heart wanted. 'I just want to say…'

Dylan fell silent as Poppy held up her hand, clearly not ready to hear what he had to say just yet. He was vaguely aware that Dr Neave had come to sit down in the seat alongside his, and that he was giving Poppy the same kind of professional smile that he'd given Dylan.

'Poppy, you clearly know Dylan, which is something that couldn't have been anticipated when we started on this journey. I think we need to take a moment to reframe the conversation.' Dr Neave spoke and Dylan resisted the temptation to tell him that calling this a journey wasn't going to make it into a walk in the park.

'This *journey*?' Poppy flashed back, and Dylan suppressed a smile. This, more than anything, convinced him that Poppy was going to be all right.

Dr Neave nodded. 'I'm sorry. You have every right to be angry and that was a bad choice of words. Shall we break for a cup of tea and see where we are in half an hour?'

'No more tea.' Poppy was beginning to sound much more sure of her ground now, and that was exactly what Dylan wanted. He turned to her, catching her gaze, and saw a warmth in her hazel eyes that he'd never stopped to notice before.

'What do you want, Poppy?'

CHAPTER TWO

WHAT POPPY ACTUALLY wanted was to be back at work. Or at home, looking forward to the time when she'd be able to hold her child in her arms, in the sure knowledge that the biological father had given her this immense gift without wanting anything in return.

But she needed to pull herself together. Despite her own horror, she'd seen the wounded look in Dylan's eyes at her dismay when she'd realised that he was the biological father of her child. Somehow, that had made him seem so much more human. Someone who could be hurt, despite all his self-assurance.

And even if what she wanted was now beyond anyone's grasp, Dylan had made a good first step in asking her. Cutting across Drs Neave and Patel's smooth assumption that they were at the centre of this decision-making process made it a *very* good first step.

'I'd like a few minutes with Dylan. To discuss this alone, please.' Poppy glanced at him, receiving a small nod. Somehow, the look in his clear blue eyes seemed to reassure her. If the eyes really were the windows to the soul, then Dylan's soul might be enough to see her through this situation.

'Poppy. Are you quite sure?' Dr Neave leaned forward in his seat, his thoughts difficult to read behind his smile. 'In a situation such as this, you should consider working with an advocate, who can act as an intermediary.' He gestured towards Dr Patel, in a signal that she might be such an advocate for Poppy.

What was Dr Patel going to do? Follow her back to the hospital and mediate in any discussions that might involve Dylan? Tell her things that she already knew about the medical and emotional implications of her situation?

Dylan leaned back in his seat, crossing his legs. Poppy glanced at him and he extended his fingers in a gesture which implied she knew all of the facts and that the decision was hers alone. Then she knew.

He might be autocratic. Irritating. Dylan's charm might follow him like a scented aura, infecting far too many of the women they both worked with. But he was honest. He made life-or-death decisions every day in the operating theatre and was aware that she had too, before her pregnancy had meant she was temporarily assigned to the less physically demanding role of post-operative care. However annoying he might be, he was the one person in the room who trusted that she could speak for herself, and appeared ready to listen.

'As I said, Dr Neave, I'd like a few moments with Dylan, please.' She heard a certainty in her voice that she didn't feel, and Dr Patel nodded, gesturing to Dr Neave that they should leave the room.

She'd made her decision now, made the first cut, and now she had to follow it through, quickly and cleanly, with every bit of the expertise she had at her disposal. Poppy waited until the door closed behind Drs Neave and Patel, then focused on Dylan.

'You knew about this yesterday?'

He nodded. 'Not that it was you. I found that out at exactly the same moment you did.'

Poppy nodded. 'I guess that a *the sooner the better* invitation to a fertility clinic is a little lower down your list of priorities if you're not eight months pregnant.' Somehow, now that they were alone, it was easier to speak her mind.

'Yeah. But when they told me *when* the mistake had taken place the situation very rapidly shot to the top of my to-do list.' He reached inside his jacket, pulling out an envelope and putting it on the coffee table. 'These are the results of my medical screening. I asked them to do a few extra tests, and to supply me with the raw data of the results, but that would have spoiled the line of my jacket.'

Surely no one was *that* vain. Poppy looked up at him and saw a self-deprecating smile. She hadn't guessed that Dylan was capable of not taking himself completely seriously. 'You don't need to do that.'

He ignored the words, and Poppy picked up the envelope. He must realise that this was the first thing she'd wanted to know. 'Now that I know you're qualified to read it, I'll make the longer report available to you.'

'Thank you. I'd like to see it.'

He nodded. 'You'll have it tomorrow.'

'I'll treat it in complete confidence, of course.' Poppy should have remembered to say that before now.

'Thanks. How do you feel about keeping all of this quiet? I understand that you may need to talk about it, but in general…' Dylan frowned.

Poppy nodded. 'I'd be grateful if you didn't say anything to anyone at work. You know how it is, tell the wrong person something and in twenty minutes everyone in the department knows. By the next morning it'll be up in Scotland.' The open lines of communication between the Great Southern in London and the Great Northern in

Edinburgh worked to good effect in many ways. One of the unintended side-effects was the unimpeded transmission of gossip.

Poppy saw Dylan turn the corners of his mouth down. She might not be guilty of spreading gossip about him, but she'd listened. Dylan never had much to say about his personal life, so how else would Poppy have known about his conquests?

'You're right. Let's keep this to ourselves, shall we? Unless, of course, there are medical issues which require disclosure, it's no one's business but our own.'

Was there a trace of vulnerability in his eyes? Or maybe Poppy was just finding that she too was susceptible to Dylan Harper's charm. Was he really trying to make a difficult situation better, or did he feel that was the best way to get what he wanted?

Now wasn't the time to think through whether she trusted him or not. That would have to come with time, and was the result of actions and not words. Suddenly Poppy felt she'd heard too many words today already.

'What do you say…? We've covered some of the basics.' Poppy pursed her lips.

'You want to get out of here?'

'Yes. I do. Unless Dr Neave has something more to say.'

Dylan's smooth composure had returned now. It was like watching water being poured into a glass, effortlessly finding its own level. 'I imagine that Dr Neave has a great deal more to say. But if you've had enough for today, then he can wait. Whatever happens next happens when you're ready, and not one moment before.'

Dylan was as good as his word. He'd ended the meeting tactfully and firmly, leaving Drs Patel and Neave as reassured as they could be in a situation like this. He wasted no time in shrugging his overcoat on and ushering Poppy through the main doors of the clinic and into the lift. As the doors closed, leaving them alone, Poppy let out a sigh of relief.

'Coffee?' He corrected his mistake quickly. 'I meant...decaf? Or herbal tea?'

Poppy smiled up at him. In the confined space, Dylan seemed very big. Very reassuring. 'Herbal tea doesn't have quite the same ring to it, does it?'

'I'll join you. I'm sure there's something to be said for it.'

'No need. If you stick with coffee, then I can at least smell it.'

He thought for a moment, clearly trying to gauge the medical ramifications of smelling coffee. 'Fair enough. Whatever gets you through the day.'

He was close, suddenly. Protective. As he ushered her out of the lift, through the lobby and into the street he seemed to move with her, always there but never actually touching her. Poppy looked to the left and then the right, wondering if she should make the decision to head for one of the half-dozen coffee shops that lined the street ahead of them, but it seemed that Dylan had other ideas. He held out his arm, in a quiet invitation for her to take it.

She was pregnant, not ill. But Poppy's legs were beginning to shake now, the third option of shock starting to take hold. She took his arm, feeling the soft material of his overcoat—cashmere, probably—and Dylan started to walk, taking the first side-street that they came to.

The coffee shop was just slightly off the beaten track, and smaller than the others. A little less shiny, but it was warm and clean. Dylan led her past the crowded counter and down three steps, into a larger, quieter room with framed posters on the walls and comfortable seating.

One of the nice little places that he just happened to know? Poppy dismissed the thought. If he *did* happen to know a few nice places where you could ask someone for a getting-to-know-you coffee, then so what? This wasn't a situation that might lead to an evening meal and then something more. They both had a different mission, and this was somewhere in the heart of the city which provided a moment of much-needed calm.

He left her to choose a seat, and Poppy made for the far corner of the room, taking off her coat and hanging it on the back of an armchair that stood next to a small table. She looked around, wondering if a waiter might appear, and he gestured towards a large blackboard on the wall which listed out the various offerings. Poppy perused the list.

'Blackcurrant and apple sounds nice...' She dragged her gaze away from the list of different coffees.

'Yeah.' Dylan didn't sound any more convinced of that than she was. 'Take a seat, I'll go and get the drinks. Anything to eat?'

Poppy still felt a little sick and shaky. Maybe... maybe not. He seemed to see her indecision. 'The croissants here are good.'

Maybe she'd feel a little steadier if she had a bite to eat. Poppy nodded, sitting down.

Dylan was gone for a while, and she could breathe now. Maybe she should make a list of things that she wanted to ask. She took a napkin from the holder on the table and a pen from her bag, and then couldn't think of anything to write.

HELP ME!

She'd doodled the words in capitals on the napkin, and then scrunched it up quickly, reaching to put it into her coat pocket when she saw Dylan reappear with a tray. This was *her* pregnancy. *Her* baby. She didn't need Dylan's help, even if every instinct was sending the unlikely message that she wanted it.

The croissants were warm and smelled great. His coffee smelled wonderful. Poppy concentrated on her mug of herbal tea, taking a sip. 'That's nice.'

He nodded, taking a sip of his coffee. 'There's something I want to tell you.'

Clearly, he'd been using his thinking time to better effect than she had. Poppy wondered whether Dylan had brought her here to deliver yet another shock, and decided that it was better to get it over with. At least she was sitting down and in the company of a medical practitioner. She took one of the croissants from the plate, putting it into her saucer and breaking a corner off it.

'I'm listening.'

'When I…' He looked around and even though there was no one within hearing distance he lowered his voice. 'When I donated my sperm, it was for one purpose. My brother and sister-in-law couldn't conceive and…'

Poppy hadn't thought of that possibility. It

seemed incongruous that a man who made no long-term commitments should have done something like that, but she was coming to the conclusion that Dylan was a nicer guy than she'd thought.

'You helped them?'

'Yes. My sister-in-law had no issues in that area, but my twin brother...'

'You're a *twin*?' Suddenly Poppy was thinking like a doctor again, and there were several very obvious questions she wanted to ask.

He took his phone from his pocket, stabbing at the small screen with his finger and then turning it towards her. Two men standing together, laughing.

'You're the one on the left?'

He raised his eyebrows in surprise. 'Yeah. Was that a guess?'

No, not really. Dylan was the one with the raw sex appeal, but Poppy wasn't inclined to give him the satisfaction of hearing that.

'I suppose I had a fifty percent chance of being right.'

He nodded. 'Sam and I are very alike, but we're fraternal twins, not identical. Since we don't share all our DNA, then it's perfectly possible for just one of us to have fertility issues.'

That was the question that was bothering Poppy. She nodded, blushing.

'Since there's already been one mix-up, it's not too much of a leap to think there could have been two. I questioned Dr Neave very closely on that when I first found out and, although they're in damage limitation mode at the moment, I believe him. And here's the proof that I *can* father a child...'

Dylan picked up his phone, scrolling through photographs. His face warmed suddenly as he found the one he was looking for and he turned the screen towards her. A little blond boy, about four years old, with a toy train.

'Oh! Look at that smile! He's very cute.' Instinct spoke before caution had a chance to modify the thought. Poppy swallowed hard. 'What's his name?'

'Thomas.' Dylan flipped the photo to one side, showing her another. 'That's him with Sam, and his wife Sophie.'

Dylan's brother had one arm around his wife and the other around his son, who was sitting on his lap. They were all smiling for the camera, but there was more than that. Every syllable of their body language showed close bonds of love.

'What a lovely picture. You and your brother *are* very alike.' Only Dylan's brother seemed happier in his skin somehow, with laughing blue eyes and less precisely coiffed hair. Maybe Poppy was over-thinking this.

Suddenly she saw the same warmth in Dylan's eyes. 'Yeah. My brother Sam is his dad, he's been with him every step of the way and I'm not sure it would be possible for him to love Thomas any more than he does. I'm his uncle, so I insist on spoiling him a bit...' He fell silent, scanning Poppy's face. Maybe he could see all of the questions forming in her head. 'Ask. Please.'

'You don't think of him as your child?'

Dylan chuckled, leaning back in his seat. 'He's my nephew and my godson. That makes him a part of me, but not in the same way that he's a part of my brother. I haven't been there when he wakes up crying in the night, or when he's sick. I can't be and it wasn't what I signed up for. I have a demanding job and my own life.'

He put everyone in their right place. Maybe Poppy was finding a place in his definition of what a family meant, but he would never think of her child as his own. She reminded herself that when she'd first realised that the biological father of her baby wasn't the donor she'd chosen she'd feared this unknown man might want to claim her child as his, and that this was exactly what she'd wanted.

'Does the rest of your family know?'

Dylan nodded. 'Yes, family and close friends. Sam and Sophie will talk to Thomas about it when the time's right, but it's not something they consider a secret. He knows who his mum and dad are.'

'And he'll know that you gave his mum and dad a precious gift?'

'Yeah. Medical science did too. And Sam and Sophie wanted a child so much—it was their determination which made it all a reality.' Dylan shrugged. 'This was one of the best things I ever did, and I don't regret anything about it.'

There was no trace of any regret in his face either. As far as his nephew was concerned, Dylan had exactly what he wanted, no more and no less. And he was in shock too. He'd never counted on his donation being used for anyone other than his own brother and sister-in-law.

And now he was a father again. *Biological* father. That one word meant a very great deal in terms of distance.

'Do you regret this?' Her fingers strayed to her stomach.

Dylan thought for a moment. 'I regret that this wasn't the way you had things planned. I don't think I have it in me to regret being part of the making of a life, though. However awkward it is, that's something that's bigger than both of us.'

Good answer. Very good answer. Poppy nodded. 'I have to admit that I didn't think I'd be sitting here drinking tea with you. We've not had a great deal to do with each other at work and…

if I'd had time to think about this, I would have reckoned on you running for the hills. But you haven't.'

'And how do you feel about that?' Dylan's gaze was focused entirely on her now.

'I'm not sure. I almost wish you *had* run for the hills.' Poppy heard a touch of defensiveness in her tone.

She could see the hurt on Dylan's face and pressed her lips together. That wasn't going to take the words back. He'd given her all of the right answers and she'd thrown the wrong one back at him.

One small part of her wished that he *had* just walked away, and that they could pretend that this had never happened. That Dylan would be the anonymous donor that she'd wanted. But the door on that option had closed behind them now, and to Poppy's surprise she'd found a kind and committed man, someone who might love her child. However complicated that was, she couldn't deny her baby that possibility.

'I'm sorry. I didn't mean it that way.' He hadn't openly reproached her, but his reaction hadn't been difficult to miss.

'It's okay. I'd rather hear what you think than what you reckon I want to hear.'

CHAPTER THREE

RUNNING FOR THE HILLS. Was that really what Poppy thought of him? She could be forgiven for that. Dylan was aware that he was capable of charming women but he never stayed around for too long.

His father had been a man who'd run for the hills, and Dylan had always felt that if he never made those promises he couldn't break them. His brother, Sam, was the product of the same broken home, and although his actions seemed very different the motives behind them were the same. Sam and Sophie's relationship was based on promises that Sam knew he could wholeheartedly keep. The brothers who were so alike in some ways and so different in others were just a demonstration of the fact that human beings weren't simply a set of predictable flow charts.

Donating his sperm had been easy with Sam and Sophie, they'd sat down together and worked out answers to every possible question in advance. He and Poppy had found themselves with a fait accompli, and if his own feelings of shock were anything to go by, she must be really struggling. A lot more than he was, and she was also eight months pregnant. Dylan only had to look at her to realise that he needed to be the one to support her, not the other way around.

'May I ask you something?' He took a sip of his coffee and then another, disappointed to find that caffeine was overrated and didn't make the question any easier.

'Yes, of course.' Poppy was still a little pink from what she clearly saw as a faux pas and Dylan wished he could get inside that beautiful head of hers. He was just going to have to be as honest as his heart would allow.

'I know you never wanted this. That you decided to bring this baby up on your own. But I can't undo what's happened or how I feel. I'd like to be there for you, as much or as little as you want. And if you'll accept me as a friend, I'd very much like to be an uncle to your child, too. Not just for birthdays and Christmas, but for whenever I'm wanted or needed.'

That didn't sound too pushy, did it? Too needy or too demanding. Poppy had lost her husband and asking whether he could be a stand-in father sounded as if Dylan was trying to take his place. He couldn't be a father, but he knew that he could be a loving and committed uncle and, if she would let him, he knew that he could promise her that.

Poppy didn't answer immediately. That was okay, she was giving it serious consideration. Dylan focused his attention on his coffee, trying not to put her under any pressure by staring.

'I guess… Since I have two sisters, there's a vacancy for an uncle that I'm looking to fill. I'm going to need someone with experience.'

Dylan felt a smile rise from his heart. 'May I send you my CV? I could provide references…'

She laughed. 'That won't be necessary. There's no salary involved and I hear that the hours can be terrible. Don't you want to think about it and come back to me later?'

'No. I'm taking the job.'

Dylan leaned back in his seat and she gave him a smiling nod. He really ought to feel more. This had been a shock and it had opened up a whole new world of commitment that he'd never asked for. But they were just echoes now, and the only thing that really gripped him was a sense of relief that Poppy wasn't going to shut him out.

It felt as if they'd settled something. Not everything, but it was more than enough for today. Poppy was sipping her tea in silence, tearing bite-sized portions from the croissant, and he reminded himself that he'd promised to let her dictate the pace.

'We're not done yet, are we.' She shot him a knowing glance. 'But I should probably be getting back to work.'

'Me too.' Dylan considered the practicalities of this next step. 'I think I'll walk, but I'll go and hail you a taxi.'

'You'd *prefer* to walk…?' She gave him an enquiring smile.

Dylan gave up. 'Maybe I'll join you and ask the driver to stop around the corner. That way, we won't be getting out of the taxi together in full view of the whole hospital.'

'Sounds like a plan.' Poppy got to her feet, putting on her coat. Apparently, sitting here while he went outside to hail the taxi wasn't on her agenda either.

She allowed him to open the door of the coffee shop for her, and as soon as she stepped out onto the pavement and raised her hand a taxi came to a stop next to them. Giving him a broad grin, she climbed in, waiting for Dylan to follow.

So this was what impending fatherhood was like. His sister-in-law had joked about his brother's over-protective attitude, and his brother had just laughed and shrugged. Sam hadn't been able to change the way he felt, and Dylan couldn't now.

As they neared the hospital he leaned forward, telling the taxi driver where to stop. When he got out, handing over a note to cover the fare and the tip, he saw Poppy wrinkle her nose and, just to annoy her even further, he asked the cabbie to take her right to the dropping-off area outside the main entrance.

They'd come a long way in just a few hours, from stunned silence, where just one word might be disastrously wrong, to cautiously teasing each other. But they were both surgeons, they knew exactly when concentration was needed, and when it was possible to step back a bit and lighten the mood. Dylan was under no illusions, there would be plenty of difficult decisions, wordless moments ahead of them.

But somehow… Somehow, he was looking forward to it. Not just the challenge of learning how to be a father, but getting to know Poppy a little better. Before now, he'd studiously ignored all of the things about her that sent tingles up his spine, but now he was noticing the light in her eyes, which changed subtly according to her mood. The way she tilted her head slightly when she smiled. The precise, graceful movement of her hands, and the burning feeling that accompanied the thought of what her touch against his skin might provoke. Dylan was trying very hard not to think about that…

'Hi, Mr Harper.' A cheery voice brought Dylan back into the here and now. One of the receptionists who manned the main desk in Neurology had clearly decided to take a late lunch hour and was walking straight towards him.

'Oh. Hey, Paul. I was miles away…' It was a little late to try and draw Paul's attention away from the taxi, which had stopped at the lights a little further down the road, but Dylan reckoned it couldn't do any harm to try. 'I don't suppose you saw any urgent messages for me this morning, did you?'

'No, just the usual stuff. I'll be back in ten minutes, but they're all in your inbox.'

'Great. Thanks.' Dylan shot Paul a smile and kept walking.

Paul was a nice guy, and everyone appreciated his cheery efficiency. Maybe he hadn't seen Poppy's red coat in the back of the taxi. Maybe he wouldn't put two and two together and come up with the right answer. Dylan just had to hope.

Poppy walked through the reception area of the hospital, deep in thought. What if the baby looked like Dylan? Had his blue eyes and blond hair? That wouldn't be so bad…

His quiet sense of humour. The way he seemed to understand what she was feeling. That smouldering look, which seemed to ignite in the face of a challenge. All good qualities, but they might make for some unexpected challenges during her child's teenage years. But they were a long way away, when just getting through today was proving a major challenge.

She'd be okay if she took this one day at a time. One decision, one thrill at the way he smiled at her. Maybe those thrills would wear off after a while and leave her alone with Nate, the one love of her life.

When she stepped out of the lift, Maisie was alone at the reception desk of the neurology department and Poppy stopped to talk. She'd seen that on TV mystery movies, people stopping to talk to someone so that they had an alibi for the time of the crime. She dismissed the thought. Neither she nor Dylan had committed any crime.

'How did it all go?' Maisie asked.

'Fine.' Poppy hadn't thought to make any secret of her visit, and her nerves at the sudden summons to the clinic must have been obvious. 'Just tying up some paperwork.'

'They haven't heard of email?'

Poppy shrugged. 'They pride themselves on their personal touch.'

She walked to her office and took off her coat. Sat down and nudged her computer into life. Funnily enough, the world still appeared to be turning, in just the same way as it had before she'd left the hospital this morning.

It was finally possible to take a breath. Close

her eyes and let her mind wander, instead of feeling that every word might provoke a catastrophe. Dylan was still there, ever present in her thoughts, but somehow his blue eyes seemed less challenging now.

What would it have been like if they'd made this baby together the traditional way? If his tenderness had turned to heat… Since Dylan wasn't here to notice the small shudder of excitement that the thought provoked, it was a risk-free fantasy. A 'what if' that had never been a part of Poppy's plan, and was seriously *never* going to happen.

She relaxed back into her chair, shifting slightly as the baby began to kick.

'Simmer down. We can do this, together.' Poppy wasn't sure whether she was speaking to herself or to her baby, but the words seemed to reassure them both.

It had occurred to Poppy, for the first time, that she didn't need to do this alone. A friend, an uncle for her baby… It all sounded a little bit too good to be true. She'd wait to find out, but while she was waiting she needed to be a bit nicer to Dylan. That comment about whether she would rather he ran for the hills had hurt him.

Nate had liked her outspokenness. He would have shrugged and told her that it wasn't the most practical option and not taken it too personally.

But then she'd chosen Nate and he'd chosen her. The way they just got each other had been a big part of the appeal.

Neither she nor Dylan had had any choice in this. They were both vulnerable, both forced into a situation that hadn't been of their making. Which brought her full circle, back to the thought that she really *did* need to be a little nicer.

Poppy leaned forward, checking her messages. This late in her pregnancy, she was confined to consultations and post-op care and she was due on the ward in fifteen minutes.

She'd spent almost two hours carefully assessing and reassuring her patients. The intense concentration that surgery took always cleared her mind of everything else, and although her temporary role was a little different it still required her full attention. When she saw Dylan making a beeline for the ward manager at four o'clock her heart almost missed a beat.

Almost. Somehow his blond hair seemed lighter, as if he'd found some sunshine hiding in a corner somewhere and brought it with him. He was clearly fresh out of the operating theatre. There must have been an emergency this afternoon which had claimed his attention. His presence here meant only one thing, that there would be a new patient coming up to the ward soon, and he had concerns about them.

Poppy looked at her watch. If she left at four-thirty then she'd miss the worst of the rush hour and get home without standing, squashed and uncomfortable, and feeling that she was about to faint in a crowded underground train. If she was going to have to work late, maybe it would be better to wait until after the rush hour had subsided a bit...

'Hey.' He was relaxed and smiling as he approached Poppy, but she could see the remains of a steely concentration in his eyes. Dylan's habit of stretching and taking a few breaths before he left the operating theatre, to shake off the stress, hadn't entirely worked this time.

'You've been operating this afternoon. Was there an emergency case?'

He nodded. 'A young mum. She was walking her older child home from school, with the younger one in a pram. They were hit by a car.'

That was bad enough news at the best of times. These days it was enough to bring a tear to Poppy's eye, and she blinked it away quickly. 'Injuries...?'

She'd tried to make that one word sound brisk and professional, but the softness in Dylan's voice told her that he saw through it. 'The baby and her big brother were fine, their mum pushed them both out of the way. She had two broken legs, and a tear in her jugular vein.'

The broken legs were the most obvious injury, but the tear to the vein in the back of the neck was the most dangerous.

'You've repaired it?'

'I was lucky to have the chance to do so. Apparently, one of the grandparents waiting at the school gate was a retired nurse, and she kept the bleeding under control until the ambulance arrived.'

'Any damage to the vagus nerve or carotid artery?' Every step of the delicate emergency surgery that Dylan had just performed was clear in Poppy's head.

He leaned forward a little, a smile playing around his lips. 'Not telling you. I'll be here and will be keeping an eye on her for a while.'

'That's *my* job, Dylan. I'm going to hazard a guess that everything went well, and there were no complications. You're not the kind of monster that jokes around if that's not the case.' Poppy pressed her lips together. Hadn't she resolved to be nicer to Dylan?

But he grinned. 'Am I the kind of monster who can persuade someone to go home on time, without too many arguments?'

'To tell you the truth, I'm rather banking on you not being any kind of monster.' Poppy realised that her hand had strayed to her baby bump and she snatched it away before anyone saw and concluded that she and Dylan were talking about her pregnancy.

'Good point. I'll do my best to convince you of it. Will you *please* go home? You could accept my promise that I'll be here for our patient, and humour me.'

Our patient. Poppy had never heard Dylan say that before. He went to extraordinary lengths for the patients that he operated on, and often seemed reluctant to give them up to someone else's care. Maybe he was getting used to the concept of shared responsibility, since he knew he couldn't just walk in and take charge of her baby.

'I could do with going home and putting my feet up for the evening. It's been an unexpected kind of a day.' This time Poppy managed to curb her tongue. *Unexpected* didn't carry quite so many value judgements as *monster*.

He nodded silently, his blue-eyed gaze catching hers. The feeling of warmth that this new connection with Dylan had started to provoke was even more inappropriate here than it had been in the coffee bar. But it just wouldn't give up, and Poppy couldn't entirely push it away.

'Unexpected for me, too. I'm hoping that we might be able to turn that into a positive.'

Poppy nodded. *Unexpected* hadn't been her favourite thing, ever since Nate had died. But she was working on that, and now might be a chance to break some new ground.

'Me too. I'll see you tomorrow.'

The emergency operation that Dylan had carried out this afternoon hadn't been quite as straightforward as he'd allowed Poppy to believe. Repairing the broken vein had been difficult, and there had been several other issues arising from the blow to the back of the woman's neck as she was thrown against the kerb. Dylan had used all of his skill, and given her the best chance he could, but she would need to be carefully monitored tonight.

Then there were the factors that had nothing to do with cold calculation, and everything to do with emotion. Faith Carpenter had two children, both far too young to do without her. Dylan had met her husband, Peter, when he'd returned to the hospital after collecting the children and taking them to their grandparents, and something about his quiet determination to do everything he could for his wife and children had touched Dylan.

Both parents wanted to be there for their kids, and that was something that Dylan hadn't had. He couldn't change that, bring his father back and make them all a happy family. But he could change this. He'd had to struggle to push that thought away more than once as he'd operated, because concentration was everything.

One of the high-care rooms on the ward had been readied, and Faith was carefully transferred into the bed. Dylan checked all her vitals, then went out to the waiting room to meet her husband, who sprang to his feet as soon as he saw him.

'I've just examined Faith, Mr Carpenter. She's sedated, but she's come through the surgery very well. We'll be keeping her under close observation tonight to make sure she continues to improve.'

'Thank you.' Peter Carpenter leaned forward, taking his hand and shaking it. 'Thank you for everything you've done. May I see her, please?'

'I'll speak to the ward manager and ask if you can go in for just five minutes. Faith will be very drowsy. She might not know you're there.'

'That's okay. I'll know it, won't I. If there's anything you could do, I'd be so grateful...'

Dylan nodded. 'Wait here. Let me go and see.'

He obtained the ward manager's blessing, and shepherded Peter Carpenter into his wife's room, after warning him that the bruises on her face looked worse than they actually were. The tears in Peter's eyes when he first saw his wife were quickly brushed away and Dylan motioned him to the chair placed next to Faith's bed.

'Hey there, darling. The doctors all say you're doing really well. The kids are both fine, they're with your mother...'

Faith's eyelids fluttered, but she didn't respond. Dylan told Peter that it would be all right to take his wife's hand, and he reached forward, gently winding his fingers around hers.

It didn't matter that Faith might not know Peter was there, because maybe she did. Suddenly Dylan could detach himself from hard facts, and hope for miracles. Maybe because a miracle was exactly what he needed. Something that might allow him to be a real father. He might have rejected the thought for all his adult life, but suddenly that was all he wanted to be. Everything he wanted to find out *how* to be.

He stepped back, picking up the notes that he'd already read and studying them, in an effort to give Peter and Faith some semblance of privacy. After ten minutes, he stepped forward again, catching Peter's attention.

'Time to go and let her get some rest. If you leave your number with Reception, we'll call you later this evening to let you know how Faith is. If she needs me, I'll be here. I'm on call tonight.' That wasn't entirely true, but since Dylan reckoned he would grab a few hours' sleep in one of the on-call rooms, it was close enough.

Peter nodded. 'I've got to go now, Faith. The doctors will look after you tonight, and I'll be here to see you in the morning. I'm going to give Andrew and Chloe both a big hug from you when I get home. We all love you…'

Dylan swallowed the lump from his throat as Peter leaned forward, kissing his wife's hand. He could usually keep this feeling under control a little better. But going home now was impossible. That was about the only solid fact that he was sure of at the moment.

CHAPTER FOUR

GET SOME REST. That was a slightly more complex procedure than it had been when Poppy had been able to fall into bed, sleep in whatever position she happened to hit the pillows, and then wake up refreshed after eight hours. But between getting home at five o'clock and leaving again at nine the following morning, Poppy had alternated between snoozing on the sofa and sleeping in her bed for a total that approximated eight hours. In between times, she'd eaten, tried not to worry and almost convinced herself that this was just a matter of her making it very clear to Dylan what was going to happen next.

That last part was the thing she was most uncertain of. Dylan was a law unto himself, talented, excellent at his job and completely unpredictable when it came to his personal life. That had never bothered her before, because she'd had nothing to do with his personal life and Dylan's approach to his job was quite different. But it mattered now. The baby that moved inside her was a part of him, too.

It wasn't unusual not to see Dylan at work, she could go for a week without catching sight of him. It *was* unusual to want to know where he was. A casual enquiry had established that he wouldn't be operating until eleven, and when she'd visited the ward she'd found that he'd been here all night. Maybe his patient hadn't been quite as well as he'd suggested, but when she'd asked about Faith Carpenter she'd found that she was doing better than expected.

Since Dylan wasn't in the cafeteria, there was really only one place he could be hiding out. Poppy tapped gently on the door of his office and then entered, wondering whether his smile might have the same effect on her that it had yesterday.

Oh! His office chair was empty, but there was an inflatable mattress on the floor which looked comfortable enough. Or maybe Dylan was just very tired, because he was fast asleep under a couple of hospital blankets. He was wearing a white T-shirt which did little to disguise a very fine pair of shoulders, and the idea of tracing her finger along the muscles of the arm that was flung across his face seemed suddenly very tempting.

'Dylan!' Her voice might be a little harsher and

louder than it really needed to be, and he woke with a start. 'Sorry…'

'Uh…' He rubbed his hand across his brow and then focused on his watch, tapping his finger on its face. 'That's okay. You beat my alarm by about ten seconds.'

'You've been here all night?' Poppy wasn't sure how she felt about the idea that he might have been covering for her.

Dylan propped himself up on one elbow, rubbing his hand across the top of his head. Blond spikes made him look more boyish.

'It's not the first time.' He looked a little apologetic. 'At least I have my own office now, which is a lot quieter and much more comfortable.'

But why? If she and Dylan stayed overnight for every patient whose future was uncertain they'd never leave the hospital. Poppy decided not to ask, because how he managed his life really was up to him.

'I'll go and fetch you some coffee, shall I?' Poppy smiled at him. That was the obvious thing to say in the circumstances.

'No, that's fine, thanks. I'll pop into the canteen and get something on my way down to the pre-op meeting, and then shower and scrub up. How did you sleep?'

'Fine. You?'

'Like a baby.'

'Good.' Poppy didn't want to discuss babies right now. Not when Dylan was looking like the guy that everyone would want to say good morning to. 'I'll get on then. Sorry to…um…'

She turned, making for the door before either of them had a chance to say anything else. It appeared that Dylan was going to get the last word, though.

'I'm not sorry. About anything,' she heard him murmur quietly as she closed his office door behind her.

Dylan was reaching new heights in working cooperatively. He'd asked whether he might pick up some lunch so that they could go through some of her notes on pre-op patient consultations together, and turned up in her office with a bright smile and a carrier bag from the local health food restaurant, which was much more tasty than anything the canteen had to offer.

He walked through into the recovery suite more often, too. Or maybe he'd always done that and Poppy just noticed when he was in the room now. He seemed to spend more time on the ward, as well, and always stopped to exchange a few words with Faith Carpenter and her husband.

He never once alluded to what bound them together. Although Poppy couldn't help feeling that the odd slip—some reference to their situation—

might be reassuring. Ever since Tuesday morning, they'd both carefully avoided the subject.

And then, on Thursday, she'd walked past the open door of his office, carrying two muffins in a bag. One of them had been intended for Kate, one of the doctors in A&E who Poppy was particularly friendly with, but when Poppy found herself stopping in Dylan's doorway it became obvious that Kate was going to have to fend for herself calorie-wise this afternoon.

'Hi. Blueberry muffin?' That was the only excuse she had to interrupt him, and Poppy held up the bag.

'Yes. Thanks…' Dylan leaned back in his seat, smiling. She couldn't go back now. Poppy walked into the office, pushing the door to behind her, half-closed to allow a little privacy, and half-open to suggest that there was nothing to see here.

He wasn't slow in picking up the signals. 'You want to talk?' Dylan asked as she sat down on the other side of his desk.

'Um… Not right now. Do you?'

He shook his head. 'No.'

Okay, then. Perhaps they'd just eat in silence, and Poppy would leave. She supposed that would be fine. She'd made her move, given him the chance to say what was on his mind, and that was going to have to be enough. She reached into the bag, aware that Dylan was watching her.

'This is one of those Sam and Sophie situations…'

Clearly, she wasn't supposed to know what that meant, and a reaction was required. Poppy raised an eyebrow, wrapping one of the muffins in a napkin and passing it to him. 'Sam and Sophie?'

'Yeah. I email Sam, telling him something, and he replies. Every time. Sophie replies when she has something to say, and the rest of the time she just assumes that I'll know that she's read it and has nothing to add.'

Poppy thought for a moment. 'They've both got points in their favour.'

He nodded. 'Yeah.'

Time to give a little something. They were relative strangers, and maybe they did need to set the ground rules that came naturally in a situation that felt this intimate.

'I think I'd probably fall into the same category as your brother Sam.'

He nodded. 'I've got a bit more in common with Sophie's style.'

Right then. Things really were as they seemed. Dylan had told her that nothing happened until she was ready, and he was keeping his promise.

He was still there, waiting for her to collect her thoughts.

'That's…good to know. Thank you.'

He grinned. Dylan's smile was still capable of reducing her to a quivering wreck, if she allowed it to. More so because she'd been noticing him a lot more recently. The way he moved. How his scrubs were always better fitting at the shoulders than at the waist, because Dylan had a great pair of shoulders. Reassuringly broad. Actually…gorgeously broad…

'Suppose I get the muffins tomorrow?'

Dylan knew exactly what was going on here. Poppy wasn't ready for another conversation right now, but she still needed some ongoing reassurance. Along with the rest of the department, she was well aware that he was a problem-solver, and that the solutions he applied in the operating theatre were both elegant and effective. She was learning that his approach to life in general added delight to the recipe.

'Sounds good. Surprise me.'

Red rag to a bull. The curl of Dylan's lip told Poppy that if it was possible to make a muffin surprising he'd do so. Before she was tempted to start flirting with him, Poppy grabbed the bag containing her own muffin and got to her feet, hearing Dylan's soft goodbye as she fled the room.

The following morning, when she opened the door of her office, the smell of warm baked goods greeted her. There was nothing on her desk but, after looking around, Poppy found a wholewheat strawberry muffin from a local bakery, behind a stack of patient leaflets on the bookshelf.

Friday sped by and then the weekend, a little easier because Poppy knew that nothing had changed and Dylan was still there. She almost couldn't wait to get to work on Monday morning, and he didn't disappoint. Poppy opened the top drawer of her desk, and the scent of a banana muffin from the health food restaurant assailed her.

She'd spent the weekend alone, and that degree of separation had helped her to think. Poppy sat down, breaking a bite-sized chunk from the muffin and savouring it for a moment. Then she picked up her phone and texted Dylan.

Dylan had waited, and Poppy had come through for him. It hadn't been as easy as he'd made out, and it wasn't all about differing email styles. He'd known she needed time to process this, and it had been hard to back away. But now Poppy had responded.

He baulked at her choice of lunch venue, though. The hospital garden was a nice place to take a walk, cool in the summer and sheltered in the winter, but it was overlooked by practically every window at the back of the building.

He texted back, hoping that didn't sound as if he was chickening out.

My office?

He received Poppy's okay to the change in plan, along with a smile emoji, and breathed a sigh of relief.

When she appeared in the doorway, at one o'clock on the dot, all the feelings he'd been trying to suppress hit him straight in the chest. He'd missed her. And now it felt that all he'd ever wanted had just burst back into his life, accompanied by a shimmer of sunshine.

Poppy was wearing a green flowery maternity top with a chunky green cardigan, leggings and comfortable flat-heeled boots. Her bright hair and eyes, accentuated by her pale skin, made a practical work outfit into something gorgeous.

'Coffee?' She was holding two cardboard beakers and placed one of them down on his desk. 'I smelled it on the way over here.'

Dylan laughed, feeling suddenly perfectly happy. Smelling his coffee without asking first seemed like an act of perfect intimacy. He stood, motioning her towards the group of comfortable chairs in the corner of the room, and Poppy sat down, depositing the drinks on the low table in front of her. He followed, closing the door as he went.

'Do you smell everyone's coffee?'

'No. Just yours.' The teasing look in her hazel eyes was there for only a moment before she turned the corners of her mouth down. 'Do you mind?'

'Not in the slightest. May I ask you something?'

'Of course. Anything.'

Dylan saw a flash of alarm in her lovely eyes. Even now, Poppy was trying to pretend that nothing had happened, and that they were just in his office chatting casually. That didn't work for him.

'Would you mind being a little less nice to me? Maybe telling me what's on your mind?'

Poppy paused for a moment, taking a sip of her tea. 'That's a big ask.'

'Yeah, I know. We're on unfamiliar ground though, and I can't imagine how you must feel about it. I'm not even sure that I can tell you how I feel, not straight away. I think we need to be honest with each other if we're going to come to an arrangement. Something that's best for the baby, and that we can both live with.'

Poppy smiled suddenly. 'Those are your priorities? Best for the baby comes first?'

'We did this. The one person that can't suffer as a result of our actions is the baby we made.'

Poppy reached forward, brushing her fingers against the back of his hand. Her touch made the hairs on his arm stand suddenly to attention. 'I like those priorities very much. It's exactly how I feel. I'm afraid I can't be any less nice about the idea.'

'That's okay.' Dylan thought for a moment. 'Why did you suggest the garden, Poppy?'

She blushed suddenly. 'You don't like the garden? It's so pretty with all the white Christmas lights in the trees. One of those secret places in the heart of London.'

Dylan nodded. 'Only it's not so secret, is it? Anyone could see us there together.'

'And sitting in your office with the door closed is more discreet?'

Dylan had to admit it felt that way. 'I close the door all the time. When I'm with a patient or a colleague that I want to discuss something with. When there's a noise outside and I want to concentrate.'

'Yes. Of course.'

'But…?' He'd say it himself if he had to but he'd rather Poppy did.

She shrugged. 'We're colleagues. Being seen together isn't really the problem, is it?'

That was as far as she seemed to want to go, but Dylan caught her meaning.

'Look, Poppy, I'm aware of my reputation…'

'Are you saying that you just have to stand next to a pregnant woman and everyone automatically thinks you're the father of her child?'

He'd asked for her honesty and he couldn't complain if it made him uncomfortable. Sometimes his own actions made him feel uncomfortable, as if he was deliberately shutting off a part of his life that he knew he couldn't handle.

He shrugged. 'I'm single and I like the companionship of women.' Her raised eyebrow told him that she knew exactly what he meant by companionship. 'I've been known to flirt, and people talk.'

He'd never flirted with Poppy. He'd felt an attraction, but that had only made him draw back. She'd been grieving, vulnerable, and he really *wasn't* a monster.

She puffed out a breath. 'This was what I wanted to talk to you about, Dylan. I'm afraid it's a little too late to stop people from gossiping.'

'Are they? About us?' This was exactly what he hadn't wanted. 'I have to admit that…last Monday…'

'Paul happened to see you getting out of the taxi. I heard.'

Dylan winced. 'I should have mentioned it. I didn't want to worry you unnecessarily. Who told you?'

'My friend Kate from A&E. Three people have asked her already if it's true that we were at the fertility clinic together last week. She said that was nonsense and that I'd gone alone, but I didn't really help matters by telling everyone that I'd just been called in to tie up some paperwork, when I got back.'

'But who does paperwork at this stage?' That sounded a little as if Dylan was finding fault, but Poppy just nodded.

'Yes, exactly. I didn't want anyone thinking that there was anything wrong with the baby, though. That would be worse.'

There *was* something worse than his being the father of her child. It was obvious, but now that Poppy had said it, an obscure feeling of happiness washed over Dylan. Not being the worst thing that had ever happened to her allowed him a little flexibility to rise to the moment.

'I'm sorry, Poppy. I really thought that we could keep this quiet.'

'Then you had your head in the sand.' Her smile told him that she was trying out the not-being-so-nice idea, and he smiled back. 'We work together. We're looking at caring for a child together…?'

She shot him a questioning look, and Dylan nodded. Yeah. If she'd let him, that was exactly what he wanted.

'I agreed with you that we should keep this a secret, because it was such a shock and I needed time to think it all through.' Poppy turned the corners of her mouth down. 'But, practically speaking, it's not going to float. What happens when you ask the pretty new nurse in Orthopaedics out on a date and then say you can't make Wednesdays because that's your babysitting night?'

'I can have a babysitting night?' That gleaming prospect was all that Dylan took from Poppy's words.

She rolled her eyes. 'I thought you wanted to be involved. That doesn't mean you just get to hold a nice clean baby.'

'I know how to change a nappy. Do you?'

Poppy laughed. 'I practised on the doll, during my antenatal classes. How hard can it be, I'm a surgeon?'

'That's what I reckoned with Thomas. My brother almost cried with laughter the first time I tried it.'

Poppy waved her hand dismissively. 'Forget nappies. I was scared that people would find out too, but I did a lot of thinking about it over the weekend and we've done nothing wrong. I wanted a baby to love and care for. You donated sperm to give your brother and his wife a very special gift. We don't have to tell everyone about it, it's not their business, but we don't need to sneak around like a pair of criminals.'

'You're happy with that?'

'Um… Well, no, not really. I might need you to remind me of what I've just said, at some point.' Poppy was fighting back now. Dylan had rejected her veil of niceness and a strong, principled and loving woman had emerged. 'But if you feel that you can own this, then so do I.'

The thought made him shiver. It wouldn't be easy because owning it gave him the opportunity to let Poppy down, the way his father had let his mother down. But although Poppy had support from friends and family, it seemed that there was no one else who would take on the role that he so badly wanted for himself.

'How do you feel about taking a quick stroll around the garden, then? Inspect the Christmas tree. Let everyone see us, and they can think whatever they like, because we really do have nothing to be ashamed of.'

She gave him a dazzling smile. 'That sounds great. I'll go and get my coat and we can get soup from the canteen and take it with us.'

* * *

It was difficult to miss Poppy's bright red coat, and the green knitted beret that was pulled down over her ears at a slightly jaunty angle. And Dylan couldn't have been more proud.

They'd taken a walk around the hospital garden, stopping to sit down and drink their soup, in full view of half the hospital. Dylan hadn't touched her once, although he'd been tempted to offer Poppy his arm. All the same, if anyone wanted to accuse them of walking slowly, or of smiling at each other under the white Christmas lights in the trees, then they were guilty as charged.

When Dylan opened the door for Poppy to enter the building, she brushed past him—or rather her coat brushed past his—without the need for either of them to flinch back.

'I had a few Braxton Hicks contractions at the weekend. I called down to Maternity and they've booked me in for a scan tomorrow, after I finish work.'

'Yes?' Dylan tried not to sound too overly excited about it. It was a routine part of Poppy's care, and she probably didn't want to turn up with him in tow. 'You're going to get pictures?'

She laughed. 'I always get as many pictures as I can, so I can spend time staring at them later.

If you're not busy, you could come along if you wanted.'

Busy? Dylan remembered that he was a surgeon and that he had a job to do. He'd temporarily forgotten what his schedule was for tomorrow…

He pulled his phone from his pocket and tried to focus on his diary entries. Poppy seemed to sense his confusion and leaned against his arm to see for herself. 'Nothing there. Unless of course you're on the ward?'

'Uh… No, I don't think so. I can always swap with someone if I am. Would it be okay with you if I… I could stay in the waiting room if you want. Perhaps you'll share some of the pictures…?'

Poppy raised her eyebrows. 'Dylan! I never would have put you down as a squeamish type. How does that work for you in Theatre?'

Maybe he should get used to asking for what he wanted, since Poppy was more than capable of answering back.

'I'd really like to come in with you and see the baby…'

She smiled up at him. 'Good. I'm really looking forward to it as well.'

CHAPTER FIVE

POPPY HAD TOLD him that there was no point in his sitting with her in the waiting room and, since he was already in the hospital, she'd phone him when she was called in for her scan. Dylan had sailed through his morning surgeries, optimism lending an edge to his concentration, and then afternoon consultations with patients who were scheduled for surgery next week. Then he'd spent thirty minutes in his office, pacing up and down, as the nerves hit him.

What if Poppy had changed her mind, when faced with the realities of having to explain his presence? That was okay, he'd be disappointed but he could handle that. He'd already told her that everything went at *her* pace and not his, and that she should do whatever seemed right for her.

But what if there was something wrong, and she was rushed down to Theatre and no one knew to inform him…? Sudden panic gripped his heart, and he was reminded of his brother's wry comment that he hadn't known what worry really was until Sophie had become pregnant. Dylan shelved the idea of emergency procedures, since that option was very unlikely, and then jumped when his phone rang.

'Busy?' Poppy's voice sounded on the line.

'No.' Dylan choked the word out.

'Hurry up, then. I've just been called in…'

Something else to panic about occurred to Dylan and he swallowed hard, telling himself that he could face a receptionist and ask which room Poppy was in, without having to explain his presence in detail. He could leave his own interest vague—no one needed to know whether he was there as a colleague, a friend or a father.

'Dylan…?'

Poppy's voice again. If he wasn't equal to this situation then what real use could he be to her?

'On my way. I'll see you in a couple of minutes.' He thrust his phone back into his pocket, stopping at the basin in the corner of the room to wash his hands. There was no real need for that, he wasn't attending this consultation in a medical capacity, but it made him feel a little better. Then he hurried down to the hospital's maternity unit.

Poppy had clearly told the receptionist that he would be coming, because she waved him straight through. He knocked on the door of the consulting room and heard a soft woman's voice calling for him to come in.

She was lying on the couch and the sonographer had switched on the scanner, ready to go. Poppy gave him a slightly nervous grin and the sonographer smiled at him, nodding towards his rolled-up sleeves.

'I don't think we'll be delivering this baby just yet. You can sit there, Dylan.'

He wasn't Mr Harper here. Dylan wasn't even a doctor, he was here with Poppy and he did as he was told. Poppy flashed him an amused look as he obediently sat down.

'Right then. Let's say hello, shall we?' The sonographer omitted the explanations about how an ultrasound scan worked, but she still provided some well-practised reassurance, noting aloud that everything looked good. That was a relief, because right now Dylan couldn't recall a single thing from his rotation to Maternity during his training and could only see the wonder. From the look on her face, Poppy felt the same.

He counted fingers and then toes. Imagined that he saw something of Poppy in the baby's features. When it moved and then settled again, he felt Poppy take his hand and realised that it had strayed to the side of the gurney she was lying on.

And... A girl. A baby daughter. The information rushed in on him and Dylan felt the last vestiges of his self-control slip away as he started to grin helplessly.

'She's beautiful. Perfect.' His voice sounded a little shaky, and Poppy turned her head towards him.

'Isn't she just.'

'And she's fine as well.' The sonographer had been concentrating on the screen and her smooth tones told Dylan everything he needed to know. 'It won't be long now, Poppy. Everything's as it should be for a delivery early in the New Year...'

Dylan didn't need to hear anything more. His gaze was fixed on the screen in front of them, taking in every second. When the sonographer pronounced herself satisfied and lifted the sensor from Poppy's stomach, all he wanted to do was to tell her to switch the screen back on and let him take a second look. Instructions to fellow medics worked in the operating theatre, but almost certainly not here.

'We're done.' Poppy nudged him. 'I'll bring the photos up to show you.'

'Right. Thanks...' Dylan gathered his wits and got to his feet. He turned to the sonographer, thanking her too, and she smiled.

'You're welcome.'

There was no hint of a question in her face. No surprise and no judgement. Dylan supposed that, like most people here, she'd seen pretty much

everything and knew how to act professionally.
If there were any rumours surrounding his accompanying Poppy, then they wouldn't be coming from her.

'I appreciate…everything.' He got to his feet,
turning quickly to walk from the room.

Poppy had followed Dylan up to his office, handing over the images from the scan for him to look
at. His face was one picture that Poppy could
scarcely drag her gaze from. All the wonder
that she'd felt as she'd watched her baby grow
in a succession of scans. The feeling when she'd
first felt her daughter move. All the ways she'd
bonded with her child, rolled up into one. Maybe
she should have brought a stethoscope with her,
just to check that he was all right, but she hadn't
expected this.

'It's a girl, then,' he murmured. 'I didn't think
to ask.'

Maybe he had, and maybe not. Poppy had
thought about telling him, and decided to find
out where he stood before she did so. Right now,
there was absolutely no question about that.

He smiled at her silence, seeming to understand. Then the pictures from the scan claimed
his attention again.

'Do you need to get back to work?' Hours
weren't really an issue, Dylan worked the same

hours she had before she became pregnant, and it was always more than they were contracted for. She was just a little worried that he might have forgotten something that he needed to do.

'No, that's fine.' Dylan shook his head. 'I was in at six this morning, and picked up a procedure that the night staff couldn't handle. I've been working through since then, there's nothing more.'

'Okay.' He'd already stared at each of the photographs three times, and that probably counted as giving him enough time to take all this in. 'I don't want to burst your bubble...'

He looked up at her. 'I hope you realise that it would take a pneumatic drill to burst this particular bubble. What is it?'

'Just a letter from the fertility clinic. You've probably got one too, but I'd like to compare notes some time.'

'I haven't heard anything from them. What does it say?'

Poppy shrugged. She'd been worried when she'd received the letter in this morning's post, but resolved to wait until after the scan to show it to Dylan. Maybe this wasn't quite the right time to discuss it, either.

'It's really nothing urgent. When you've got a minute tomorrow...'

He looked up at her questioningly. Then Dylan

chuckled. 'I can't pretend I'm not putty in your hands at the moment, and you could probably get me to agree to anything. We may have to put a coping strategy in place for that, so it'll be good practice if you show me the letter now.'

It was difficult to tell whether he was joking or not and Poppy decided not to enquire, since Dylan might not know the answer either. She took the letter from her handbag and slid it across the desk towards him.

'I want your opinion. Not just a *whatever you want*, please.'

He nodded, his face hardening as he read the letter through.

'My opinion? You're sure?'

'Yes, Dylan.' Poppy felt a quiver of uncertainty. Dylan hadn't put a foot wrong so far, which was more than she could say for herself. It suddenly occurred to her that this might be the exception to that.

'Well, for starters, I think that writing to you just weeks before you're due to give birth shows more concern for themselves than for you. Putting that aside, my preference would be that neither of us signs anything. Do you need the money?'

'Of course not.' A surgeon's salary was a lot more than enough for Poppy's lifestyle and she'd thought very carefully about all of the costs involved in bringing up a child.

'Okay. Then a confidentiality agreement is going to give you nothing. The fertility clinic— or, more likely, their lawyers—are probably worried about the newspapers and so on, but what if you wanted to tell someone? A friend, or maybe someone you have a relationship with at some point in the future? Someone who's advising you about your own needs or those of your child?'

'I'm not intending on starting another relationship…' Dylan was right in every other respect.

'And I wasn't intending this. It's happened, and now I wouldn't undo it for the world.' His expression softened suddenly and he glanced again at the photographs on his desk, before resuming the brisk pace of the discussion.

'We decided that we aren't going to sneak around, or feel that this is some kind of guilty secret. If that's what you want, then don't sign the confidentiality agreement, however much they offer you as a *"gesture of good faith"*. I'm your child's biological father and that means I can make those kinds of gestures, too.'

For a moment Poppy wasn't quite sure what he meant and then it hit her. She recoiled from the thought. 'I said that I don't need money. Not theirs or yours…'

'Okay.' He held his hands up in surrender. 'I know. I'm just saying.'

'And the other contract?' Poppy hardly dared ask now.

'I'm all for that. You entered into this on the basis that the biological father would have no parental responsibilities or rights over your child, which is a standard arrangement. As such, your rights over your child are probably protected, but I'd be keen to sign a document which confirms this and shows that I understand the legal situation. This is not me running for the hills, by the way, I just want you to retain control.'

'I get that.' Poppy felt a wave of relief that she hadn't realised she'd been waiting for. 'So you think we should ask them to draw up those documents and sign them?'

'I'd like to suggest something a little different. When I donated sperm for Sam and Sophie we had an independent solicitor, who specialises in family law, draw up a contract. We'd already agreed everything between us but…' Dylan shrugged. 'It was really important for us to know exactly how the family relationships were going to work and for us to all feel secure about our roles. Knowing that Sophie and Sam are Thomas's real parents allows me to get the most out of being an uncle.'

'No. It's sensible…' Poppy could never have

anticipated sitting here, having this conversation. Having a baby with anyone other than Nate... A paralysing wave of guilt hit her. She'd wished Nate might be there for all of her other scans, but when she'd seen the look on Dylan's face she'd thought of no one but him.

'We can instruct anyone you choose, but the solicitor that we used is very good and made sure that the document we signed exactly reflected everyone's wishes. And in case you're wondering, she isn't cheap but she's the best. I'll be covering her fees.' Poppy opened her mouth to protest and Dylan shook his head. 'I want everything to be as you intended it, Poppy. This is a cost that you hadn't anticipated, and I'm going to insist.'

'You're being very reasonable about all of this.'

He laughed, leaning back in his chair. 'This is what I want, Poppy. Now you have to take a few days to think about it, and tell me what you want.'

'I don't need a few days. You're right about everything, apart from paying the solicitor's fees.'

'Okay, I'll reserve the right to disagree with you on both of those points. Sleep on it, and tell me again in a couple of days, because this is something that affects the rest of our lives and it's important. We can resort to pistols at dawn

over the solicitor's fees later.' He planted his el-
bows on the desk, leaning forward. 'How did
we do?'

'I think we handled it pretty well. Why don't
you come over to my place at the weekend for
lunch, and we can make a final decision then?
Unless you have anything else planned?'

'Nothing planned. Thanks, we'll do that. My
car's in the staff car park, so I'll give you a lift
home this evening. You don't want to be on the
Tube during rush hour.'

No, she really didn't. Poppy had been reck-
oning on a taxi home. 'Don't you want to scan
those photos first?'

He grinned, nodding. 'Do you have a scanner?'

Poppy pointed to the printer on his desk. 'You
have a scanner, Dylan. That doesn't just print
things, it scans them as well.'

'Does it? You want to show me how to do that?'

'Dylan! You don't know how to use your own
scanner?'

He grinned at her. 'My nephew tells me that
a four-year-old is better with this kind of thing
than I am. He should know, since he *is* a four-
year-old.'

Poppy had saved the scans onto Dylan's phone,
wondering whether he'd look at them again tonight. She couldn't help hoping that he might.

She had *someone*. The person whose number you gave when anyone asked if there was someone they could call. Someone who came into work at six in the morning, bringing his car, so that she didn't have to make her way home with the regular crowds that flooded into busy London stations every evening. That person who she'd show a problematic letter to, and who could come up with an answer that she was comfortable with. Someone who might love her child in the same way she did—maybe not quite as much, but who might just feel from time to time that their baby daughter was his first priority...

No. She'd gone too far. Nate had been her *someone*, the person who'd always put her first. She might feel that Dylan would do that, but perhaps every woman he'd been associated with—and there were a lot of them—had felt the same way. That was his charm, his appeal. Poppy was getting carried away, forgetting that this baby was the one that she and Nate had never been able to have. She didn't really belong with Dylan and neither did her child, it had all been an accident that was never meant to happen.

All the same, when he'd suggested they go and get something to eat, because the roads would be crowded at this time in the evening as well, she'd agreed. That was just a practicality. And when she'd wondered aloud whether they might stroll up to one of the stores in either Oxford Street or Regent Street, to pick up some Christmas gifts for her nieces, his reaction was clearly one that moved beyond the bounds of putting time on their hands to good use.

'You want to take me to a toy store?' He was grinning like a four-year-old.

'Can't you go in on your own? Or are you worried about getting lost?'

Dylan chuckled. 'A second opinion's always good. I'm still deciding what to get Thomas for Christmas. How many nieces do you have?'

'I'm only buying for my middle sister's two girls. Our oldest sister lives in Germany so her son and daughter's presents are all sorted.'

He nodded. 'So you won't be seeing them at Christmas?'

'No, they're going to her husband's family. My mum and dad, along with my middle sister and her family, are going over to stay with her in Cologne for a couple of weeks before Christmas. I dare say they'll be doing a tour of the Christmas markets for some presents. They'll be back the day before Christmas Eve and we'll have Christmas together.'

'You're buying for two girls, then? Any ideas yet?'

'The eldest is quite sporty and my sister says she needs a new kit bag, so I'm going to get her that. The younger one likes taking things apart and putting them back together again, so I thought I'd get her one of those sets of bricks that you can put together to make something that works.'

Dylan's brow creased. 'Okay then, a store with a sports department *and* a toy department...'

'What about Thomas—what are you thinking of getting for him?'

'Uh...no idea. I usually just go and play with everything and see what catches my eye. I'm slightly behind on that this year.' Dylan thought for a moment. 'I'll just come and play with the bricks, shall I?'

She was seeing a whole new side of Dylan, one that he kept carefully hidden at work. And it was a really nice side, carefree and buoyant. Christmas shopping suddenly seemed like a new adventure.

'Okay, then. I'll buy and you play.'

He sprang to his feet. 'Sounds good. Hurry up and get your coat, then...'

CHAPTER SIX

DYLAN HAD OFFERED his arm for the short walk
to Oxford Street, and Poppy had taken it. When
the relatively quiet backstreets opened up onto
bright Christmas lights and crowds in the main
thoroughfare he became protectively close, and
Poppy didn't draw back. It was nice to have
someone with her, even if Dylan could never be
the someone.

It appeared that he was intent on inspecting
all the children's sports bags thoroughly, sliding
his hands into the pockets, turning them inside
out and fiddling with the straps. But a smiling,
'Decision, Mr Harper!' snapped him back into
work mode for a moment, and he pointed to the
style that Poppy had thought might be best.

'That one.'

'I agree. What do you think of the dark pur-
ple one?'

He nodded. 'Yeah. That's nice.'

Job done. Poppy took a reusable carrier bag
from her pocket and unrolled it, giving it to the

cashier who was dealing with her purchase, and Dylan retrieved it from the smiling woman. Just a man carrying his pregnant partner's bags. They must see that all the time over Christmas, but it sent a shiver down Poppy's spine.

When they got to the toy department, he slid the bag over his shoulder to leave both his hands free. His eyes had lit up like warning signs and he was looking around with an expression of dazed wonder on his face. Poppy took his arm, propelling him over to a large display of toy bricks, before he got caught up with anything else.

'This is wonderful...' He leaned forward, turning one of the moving circular arches of a space station with his finger.

'It is, isn't it. But it's a bit too complicated for Anna, I think. It'll drive my brother-in-law crazy trying to help her put it together.' Poppy moved on, pulling Dylan with her.

She decided on a smaller model of a water mill, which had moving parts that transferred water from one container to another. Since Dylan had played for a while with the display model, it would probably suit little Anna too. She nudged him in the ribs and he jumped, grinning.

'Hey. You want to look at some more of these? For your nephew?'

'You think he'd like one? I could mention it to Sophie.'

The answer to his question was obvious. If the boy was anything like his biological father, then yes, he'd love one.

'Can you give her a call and ask her?'

'Right. Yes, good idea, I can show them to her.' He manoeuvred Poppy into a seat beside the display, which someone had just vacated, and fiddled with his phone, speaking loudly over the hubbub around them.

'These are the ones…'

Poppy rolled her eyes. This might take a while, but she was sitting down and she didn't have to worry about bags or trains home. Dylan turned the phone around and she caught a glimpse of a laughing woman with dark hair.

Maybe she should have looked the other way, pretended that she wasn't with Dylan. But his sister-in-law probably wouldn't think twice about seeing Dylan with an unknown woman, and the screen was moving too fast and probably not big enough to reveal her pregnancy bump. Poppy reminded herself that she was *accompanying* Dylan and not *with* him.

He pointed the phone towards the display, carefully panning around to take in as much as possible. Then a few spoken words and he nodded, ending the call.

'Sophie says she thinks he'll love something like this. His birthday's in March and they were thinking of getting him one then, but Christmas is fine. She said I could help him put it together.'

Poppy nodded. Dylan hadn't just chosen something, he'd asked first. If this was a blueprint for the way he intended to go with their daughter, the arrangement would be fine with her.

'Did she say which one?'

'No.' Dylan frowned. 'She couldn't see them all that well, so she's left me to decide.'

'Well, you can start with the ones that have his age range printed on the box. Then pick the one you think he'll like the best. I'll stay here for another minute or two.' Or maybe three. The shop was crowded, but the seats were placed in such a way that she could see the display without being jostled.

'You don't mind?'

'No, take your time.' Poppy was starting to enjoy this. Dylan's excitement and the boyish look on his face. Even his indecision, which was never part of his persona at work, made her smile.

'Thanks…' His gaze turned towards the space station, lingering on it for a moment, and Poppy shook her head. That would be for ten to twelve-year-olds, at least.

* * *

Forget champagne. He was with an intoxicatingly beautiful woman and this was one of the best evenings that Dylan had spent in a long while. He'd done something practical, and got Thomas a present that both he and Poppy agreed that he'd love. Sam would understand how much that meant to Dylan. Their father had always considered that any effort on his part should produce tangible results, and when he'd gone to live with his divorced lover and her daughter, all of his time and money had been spent on them. Dylan and Sam's mother had struggled, and everyone had to understand that Christmas wouldn't be the same.

Things were different now. Their mother's car was beginning to show its age, and he and Sam had bought her a surprise gift of a shiny new runaround. Christmas at Sophie and Sam's place would be everything that a family Christmas should be—full of warmth and tradition, with presents for everyone under a huge tree. That was the way that Sam dealt with it all, but Dylan hadn't been able to forget so easily.

But somehow, he'd forgotten when he was with Poppy. Her smile, the baby inside her. That was what Christmas was all about. But there was the glitter too, and the excitement of buying presents. He'd picked up a catalogue so that he could

study the full range of construction kits in detail
at home, and they'd stopped to get some wrapping paper on the way to the rooftop café.

It was a little chilly for Dylan's taste, but it
seemed to suit Poppy's current temperature
gauge perfectly. And the view was spectacular,
with Christmas lights spread out below them as
far as they could see.

'What's that?' She meandered towards some
activity that was going on in a darkened corner of
the space, and Dylan followed with the tray. Suddenly the white painted walls glowed with light
as someone started to fiddle with some equipment on a small table.

'Ah—I see, it's a star projector. Do you want
to sit here?' He indicated a nearby table.

'Yes, please.' Poppy plumped herself down,
mesmerised by the display. Dylan couldn't drag
his gaze from the look on her face, and almost
spilled her herbal tea as he unloaded the tray.

'Would you like a leaflet?' A young man approached them. 'The stars are all absolutely correct and you can get different filters that give
you the view from different parts of the world.'

Poppy laughed. 'Any spaceships?'

'Um… I don't think so. I can check…'

'No, that's okay. We've got a spaceship construction kit already.' She glanced at Dylan and

he nodded. One spaceship at a time, and the projector seemed a little too advanced for Thomas.

'It'll do a few other things. There's a filter that does snowflakes, which looks great on a wall. Maybe for the baby?' The young man was clearly covering every sales point that occurred to him, and Dylan smiled, leaving Poppy to correct him.

'Newborns can't see as far as a wall, they're very short-sighted. But I'll take a leaflet if you don't mind. To think about for next year, maybe.'

'Have a great Christmas.' The lad brightened at the idea of a willing recipient for his leaflets and gave one to Poppy and an extra one to Dylan before moving on to the next table.

'It's not really for kids, is it.' He glanced at the leaflet. The price and the assertions about the scientific accuracy of the projection made the gizmo an adult toy.

'No. It's gorgeous though, isn't it. Imagine going to sleep under the stars.'

Dylan chuckled. 'Maybe it *does* work on babies. If you're calm and happy then that rubs off on them, doesn't it?'

'That's an excuse, Dylan.' She looked up from her copy of the leaflet. 'However much I like the idea, I'm not going to fall for it. I've got far too many things to get for the baby as it is.'

Right now, Dylan wasn't thinking of the baby, he was thinking about Poppy and he so wanted her to have something nice for herself. But it was far too soon to offer. Maybe next year, when they'd agreed what he could and couldn't do and he'd shown that he could stick to that. That was killing him right now, but he had to show Poppy that he was going to do this the right way. The way *she* wanted it to be.

'Why don't you get one for yourself?' Poppy grinned at him.

'Nah. I'd never get to see it. I fall asleep the moment my head hits the pillow.'

She gave him a fleeting look of disbelief, quickly hidden by a smile. She was right. If Dylan had company for the night, he never allowed himself to be the first to fall asleep. But stargazing was different. Part of a relationship that was entirely different to the ones he usually had with women, and which had to be made to last.

'Are you warm enough?' Poppy was undoing the buttons of her coat and loosening her scarf.

'Yeah, I'm fine.' Dylan decided that he could at least take his gloves off, because his coffee was hot. And sitting here, amongst stars and Christmas lights, was one of those special moments that he wouldn't miss.

Neurology was busy. The approach of Christmas didn't allow any let up in emergency patients, and the pressure to treat those who were scheduled for operations wasn't any less either. But people wanted to take leave, to sort out their own Christmases, and that left all of the remaining staff working to capacity.

'No!' She heard Dylan's voice as she passed the open door of the surgical office. 'One of my usual team is away today and another two have been co-opted onto other teams. I know we're busy, but I'm really not confident that I can give this patient the best care without a full team. I'm going to need another surgeon present.'

'I understand all that, Dylan, really, I do. But I can't magic a surgeon up out of nowhere.' The surgical co-ordinator's voice sounded stressed. Paula had a difficult job at the best of times, everyone wanted the best for their patients and human resources were always the most valuable commodity.

Guilt, at being one of the surgeons who *wasn't* available, stopped Poppy in her tracks. Then she thought again. She walked into the office, scanning the board. The department *was* unusually busy today, and Paula was quite right.

'I'm a surgeon.' The obvious answer sprang to her lips and she tried to qualify it with a joke. 'Not a bad one, actually.'

Dylan turned. 'No, Poppy. You're one of the best, but we have a patient coming in by ambu-

lance with extensive head trauma. From what I'm
told, it'll be a complex operation and you can't
be expected to stand for that long.'

'So get me a stool.' She turned to Paula. 'Not
one of the little ones, something a bit more sup-
portive... You know what I need.' Paula had
three kids of her own.

'Yeah, okay. If you're sure?'

Dylan opened his mouth to answer, but Poppy
beat him to it. 'Yes. Thanks, Paula.'

Paula hurried away, leaving her to face Dylan's
wrath. That felt like a challenge Poppy could rise
to suddenly.

'I'm not happy with this, Poppy. I'm not prepared to put one person at risk to help save another. I'll find someone else.'

'Who?' Poppy gestured towards the board.
'There are plenty of surgeons up there who are
doing something else. And one standing in front
of you who isn't.'

Doubt showed in his eyes. Dylan was clearly
agonising over this decision, and it wasn't one
that Poppy would have liked to make for someone else either. But he didn't have to make her
choices for her. He didn't have the right...

'Mr Harper. You need a surgeon?'

'Yes, but...'

Poppy shot him her best *Don't you dare* look,
and he fell silent.

'Then I'm perfectly capable of making this decision. Go downstairs and wait for the patient to arrive and do an initial assessment. I'm going to go and get ready, which might take a little longer than usual because I can't reach my feet. My hands are, however, at your disposal.'

Dylan tried one more imploring look and Poppy ignored it. 'Yes, Ms Evans.'

'Paula's put it down for Theatre Three?' Poppy glanced at the board. 'I'll see you there.'

'Poppy…' Dylan caught her arm. 'If you feel under stress you have to stop. Please.'

'Dylan, you don't have to worry about me. I know what all the risk factors are, and this is well within my capabilities. If I do find myself in difficulties, I'll tell you. But, in the meantime, I know I can help. Is that all right with you?'

His gaze searched her face and he gave a brisk nod, before turning to hurry away.

Poppy could have handled that better. She was confident that she could assist Dylan, and she could have taken him to one side and acknowledged his fears. Maybe pointed out that in the best of all worlds she shouldn't be in the operating theatre, but not every situation had to be ideal to make it workable. But pride, and the rigid determination she'd had from the start, that this was *her* pregnancy and she could do it alone, had got in the way.

By the time she'd finished scrubbing up, the team was already assembled. Paula had done a good job, and found a surgeon's stool with a backrest from one of the other theatres. Poppy nodded to the rest of the team and took her place, sitting quietly amidst the focused activity. She needed to save her strength, and then everyone would get through this just fine.

Dylan arrived, and gave her a guarded nod. And then the patient was brought in and lifted onto the table.

He was right. No one person could do this alone. A crushed skull, major bleeding—this kind of injury was going to leave its mark and it was their expertise that would dictate how much of a mark.

'Right then. I'm going to start with the major injury, here.' He indicated the mass of blood and shattered bone on one side of the patient's skull. At least his head was already shaved, and Poppy thanked their lucky stars for that sartorial choice.

'I need you to assist and also keep an eye on the other injuries. There will be times when I can manage on my own, and when I ask you to take a break, that's exactly what you do.' She saw his eyes lighten in a smile. 'Got it, Ms Evans?'

'I've got it. If I feel I need to take a rest, I'll

give you as much warning as I can. Got that, Mr Harper?' Poppy grinned back at him. They'd disagreed but that was forgotten now.

'Yep.' He looked up, his gaze moving around the assembled team. 'Okay, everyone. We'll take half an hour to see what's what, and then we'll have some music, shall we?'

Poppy would never have put Dylan down as a lover of classical music, his body was made for wilder rhythms. But somehow the soft strains of Bach seemed to suit his precision. The music wasn't loud enough to intrude on the constant to and fro between them, but just enough to help focus their concentration.

'Can you see how far that sliver of bone is embedded?' Once the mess of impact had been cleared, the patient's brain was relatively free of injury, but there was still a long way to go.

'No. It may be deep…' Poppy pointed to the chart that was being updated as each piece of bone was extracted. With shards this small, it was difficult to tell whether they'd got everything or not.

'That's what I'm thinking. See that gap, right there…' Dylan stopped to study the chart. 'I'm going to take another scan and do some exploratory work. Comfort break, Ms Evans.'

'I could do with one, Mr Harper. I'll be back in half an hour?'

'Make it forty-five minutes.' The use of their surnames was becoming a private joke between them, somehow more intimate than the use of first names. And there *was* intimacy between them now. The understanding of two people who'd found they could work well together, each anticipating the other's every move. There was no manufacturing it. Sometimes it happened in Theatre, and sometimes it didn't. Everyone knew that you accepted it for what it was, and made the most of it when it did happen.

How did he do it? Poppy needed more rest than usual, and Dylan had made sure she took it, but he'd worked without a break. Concentrating for hours on end, performing the most delicate work under both mental and physical stress. Even the strongest and fittest of surgeons needed to take time out during a long procedure, but Dylan seemed tireless.

'Nice one.' He'd carefully extracted the last piece of bone from their patient's brain, and Dylan stood back, flexing his shoulders. 'Don't you need a break, Mr Harper? I'll stay and keep my eye out for any bleeding.'

He thought for a moment. Dylan might push

himself, but he wasn't rash, and his patient always came first. 'Ten minutes, Ms Evans.'

'Make it fifteen,' she called after him. 'I'm not going to need you back before then.'

Dylan reckoned that every woman he'd known had taught him something. That was broadly true, although recently there hadn't seemed quite as much to learn. Or maybe he just wasn't so interested in learning it. But this was ridiculous.

Poppy made him feel like a raw recruit in the theatre of life. She was vulnerable and in a bad situation, and she seemed at a loss sometimes. But she still knew how to be strong and she definitely had no difficulty in making her voice heard.

She'd been right when she'd snatched the right to decide whether she could go into Theatre back from him. But she had the grace to know that Dylan had only been trying to protect her and acknowledge that too.

'Okay. I think that's everything now. We'll close?' Having Poppy to refer to at every stage had made him strong. Someone who could see what he saw in a situation and pull him up if she saw something he didn't.

'Yes, I agree. You're going to use a temporary implant?'

Dylan nodded. It would take time to make a

new prosthetic covering for the brain and it was necessary to protect it in the meantime. Poppy watched while he carefully finished their work and dressed the wounds. Then he stood back.

'Go well, Craig.' Poppy murmured the words as the patient was wheeled out of the operating theatre. Dylan probably had seen his name written on the board, but he'd taken no notice. He turned to her with a smile and Poppy shrugged.

'They can't hear me, obviously. I just say it.'

Nice. Dylan stretched his aching limbs, wondering if he might come up with a version of it. Something like Poppy's, although he wouldn't steal her exact words.

'Oh.' He heard her catch her breath and looked round. Poppy was leaning forward slightly, clearly trying not to make a fuss.

'Braxton Hicks?' He tried to make the enquiry sound casual.

'Yes. They go pretty quickly and it's not like a proper contraction. More like menstrual cramps.' She looked up at him, grinning. 'You don't have much of a reference point there, do you.'

'No. But I get the general gist of it. Come on. Time to get back to your office and put your feet up. I'll finish up here, and then take you home.'

'I've been sitting down all afternoon…' Poppy slid to the edge of the stool and seemed to stumble slightly as she put her weight onto her legs. Dylan caught her, holding her tight.

'Okay. I've got you.' There were still a few people left in the operating theatre, checking equipment and cleaning up. That made no difference. Dylan wasn't letting go of Poppy.

'So you have. I'm okay, my leg went to sleep.'

'All right, then. Just start walking and I'll stick around until it wakes up.'

Poppy didn't put up a fight. She seemed wobbly and suddenly tired, beyond just pins and needles in her leg, and she clung to him as he supported her to the doors, which swished open as he punched the control. It was the sudden fatigue that hit almost everyone after a long operation was concluded, and Poppy was experiencing it more acutely than usual.

He took her into the de-gowning area and sat her down. She looked up at him, pressing her lips together. 'I suppose you can say it now.'

'What? I told you so? You're the one who proved me wrong. I couldn't have done that procedure without you and you were right, we made it work.'

She grinned. 'Okay. I don't mind if you're nice to me.'

That was a relief, because Dylan didn't have much time. He had to check that Intensive Care had all the information they needed, and then go and see the patient's relatives. Craig's relatives.

'I have to go…' He didn't need to explain all that to Poppy and she nodded. He looked around, seeing the medical student who had been present during the operation.

'Candace, would you help me out, please, and sit with Ms Evans until I get back? Whatever you do, don't let her persuade you that she's okay and you don't need to stay.'

'No, Mr Harper. You can count on me.' Candace sat down next to Poppy.

Poppy raised her eyebrows. 'Don't worry about me, I'm not going to move a muscle. I'll take Candace through some of the points she may have missed during the operation.'

Dylan chuckled. Poppy was unstoppable, and he certainly wasn't up to being the immovable object that could change that. Candace was grinning from ear to ear at the prospect of a senior surgeon's undivided attention for half an hour.

'Great. Good idea.'

CHAPTER SEVEN

POPPY HAD TIDIED up a bit, and even gone to the lengths of giving her flat a more thorough vacuuming than it had received in the last few weeks. Two weeks till Christmas, and with another three weeks to go of her pregnancy, she was suddenly feeling heavier. Maybe she was going to have to take her mum up on the offer to come round for a couple of days when she got back from Germany and help with a spring clean.

All the same, the place looked okay in the low winter sunshine, which slanted through the south-facing windows. It was the first thing she and Nate had seen about this flat—the space that was large enough for a seating area at one end and a dining area at the other, and the way that it flooded with sunlight in the late mornings and early afternoons.

She'd put her laptop, along with a pad and her list of talking points, on the dining table as a nod to the strictly business tone of the morning. Dylan would be here soon, and when he'd said that he could book a conference call with the solicitor who had handled his own agreement with his brother and sister-in-law, Poppy had agreed. It was a nice touch that a family lawyer arranged meetings with people out of work hours and in their own homes, and Poppy hoped that she'd like Vera Chamberlain. Or…she didn't really need to *like* her, just to feel comfortable with her advice.

The doorbell sounded and Poppy picked up the remote, buzzing Dylan in and telling him to come to the sixth floor and turn left. When her own doorbell sounded, she released the lock to let him into the flat.

'Through here,' she called to him and when he appeared in the sitting room Poppy gave him a welcome smile from her armchair. Dylan shed his padded winter jacket and draped it over the back of the sofa, clearly more than happy to shift for himself.

'Glad to see you're putting your feet up today.' He grinned at her. Blue eyes, broad shoulders and the subtle scent of something gorgeous. Poppy tried not to think about any of that.

'Would you like something to drink?' She slid to the front of her seat, ready to stand, and he shook his head.

'Why don't you stay there? If you point me towards the kitchen, I can make the drinks.'

'On the other side of the hallway, back towards

the front door. Thanks, mine's a blackberry and apple, please.' Dylan turned and she called after him. 'There are biscuits and some cake in the second cupboard on the left...'

'I'll manage.' He disappeared, leaving the door open, and she heard the sound of kitchen doors opening and closing. Poppy couldn't resist picking up her phone...

'Whoa...'

She heard his exclamation of surprise as the coffee machine started up. Then he appeared in the doorway.

'Is that a robot coffee machine, or just a freak lightning strike?' He pretended to frown at her laughter.

'There's an app.' She held up her phone. 'I filled the machine before you got here.'

'In the interests of scaring the guy who only uses his phone for telephone calls and the odd photograph?' Dylan was taking it pretty well, grinning broadly now.

'It wasn't premeditated. It only just occurred to me.'

'That makes it okay, then. Crime of passion. Is the kettle going to attack me if I reach for it?'

'You don't need to reach for it, it'll be boiling in...' Poppy picked up her phone, fiddling with it '...one minute. My sister gave me some automatic plugs that you can control with an app for

Christmas last year. It's surprising how handy they've become all of a sudden.'

'So if I were to ask whether you want biscuits or cake, do I need to duck while a knife flies across the room?'

'Sadly not. A couple of the lemon cookies would be nice. There's ginger cake in the cupboard as well...'

'Cookies are fine.' He turned back towards the kitchen. 'I'll stick with the no-knives option, just in case...'

Dylan returned with the drinks and sat down. The stupid practical joke, played on a whim, had worked to break the ice. It had been nagging at the back of Poppy's mind that this was the flat that she and Nate had bought together, and now Dylan was here to talk about the baby that she'd wanted with her husband. But she had to face things as they were today, not as they had been.

'Your flat's great. Really roomy for one person...' He pressed his lips together suddenly, as if he'd just realised that he'd said the wrong thing.

'It's okay. You can ask.'

He considered the option for a moment. 'Not my place. Maybe the answer will come up in conversation at some future date.'

Dylan wasn't pushing, although he must want to know. It occurred to Poppy that it was probably just as difficult for him to come here as it was for her to play host.

'This was the flat that my husband and I bought when we got married. When he died I felt that I couldn't leave, but I didn't really want to stay either. So I decided to wait a while to see how I felt when I got over the shock.'

Dylan nodded.

'I had counselling before I started with the fertility clinic, and that was one of the things I discussed. I don't want a shrine to my husband, I want a home. I had the place redecorated and replaced some of the furniture—the mortgage was paid off by the insurance policy we'd taken out. Nate's still in my heart, but I've made sure that there are no ghosts here any more.'

'That's… It sounds like a good place to be.' He shot her a look which implied several gentle questions.

'It does, doesn't it. I still have my moments but… I just don't want you to think that your being here is making things difficult for me.' That was a little aspirational as well, but it was where Poppy wanted to be. Where she *was* for most of the time.

'To tell you the truth, I was wondering. It's really not my intention to try and take anyone's place, because I know I can't.'

'We'll find our own places, Dylan.'

He nodded. 'Is it my place to notice that you don't appear to have a great deal in your fridge?'

'I sent you into the kitchen, so I can hardly say *no*, can I?' All the same, Poppy wished he hadn't. This sudden slowing down had caught her unawares and she was a little embarrassed. 'I'm buying little and often at the moment.'

'Make a list. I'll go out and get some shopping, after we've spoken with Vera.'

No *Would you mind* or *If you want*. Dylan had taken everything she'd said on board, and Poppy was in no position to argue if he was exploring a little, to find out what his place might be. She didn't much want to argue, because a line of shopping bags on the kitchen counter sounded like pure heaven at the moment. Independence could wait until after the baby was born.

Vera had explained everything to them, and Dylan was pleased to see that her common sense and down-to-earth approach obviously impressed Poppy. Then came Vera's questions, which in Dylan's experience were generally very much to the point.

'Dylan, I'm seeing an inconsistency here. On one hand you're keen to sign an agreement that gives you no rights or responsibilities. But you also say that you wish to be a part of this child's life.'

'I need to earn that.' Dylan realised that this was the first time he'd said it so bluntly. In the window that displayed their images on the screen, he saw Poppy turn suddenly, and look at him.

'You don't think you already have?' Poppy's murmured words felt like a dagger of sunlight, plunged straight into his heart.

'It takes longer than a few weeks.'

This was what he needed. If he could prove himself then he wouldn't feel so guilty about hoping that Poppy would want to give a little more.

Vera pursed her lips, clearly setting the matter aside for the moment. The opinion on the confidentiality agreement was more straightforward, and Poppy spoke for them both. Once Vera had reassured herself that Dylan felt the same way, she told them that she would write to the clinic on their behalf and deal with the matter. End of story. She added her own warm wishes for the baby, told a joke about the birth of her first child, who was now a father of two himself, and they were left with the image of her smile as she briskly ended the video call.

Poppy leaned back in her seat, rubbing her back. 'Nice lady.'

Dylan nodded. 'Yeah. She can be ferocious when she wants.'

Poppy laughed. 'Oh, I got that. Are we sure that we want to set her on the clinic? They've been really good to me...'

'She'll handle it. Vera knows how to apply a velvet glove approach—the iron fist only appears if she sees her clients being bamboozled into something.' Dylan valued Poppy's instinct to be kind, but she needed to stop worrying. 'We're not on our own with this any more, Vera will come back to us and propose a way forward.'

'Yes. Good.' Poppy got to her feet, walking over to the sofa and sitting down, a look of pure bliss on her face. Dylan caught up her writing pad and a pencil from the table.

'Now we can worry about the list, eh? Or shall I just visit the kitchen again and look in all your cupboards?' The smiling threat was enough to make Poppy comply, and she started to reel off a list of everything she needed.

Poppy ordered the list in food groups—fruit, vegetables, dairy... That was probably the order that Dylan would find them in the local supermarket she'd suggested as well. But she'd missed out one thing...

'Anything for Christmas? Before the shelves empty out?'

She shook her head. 'No, that's all sorted. Mum's already got everything organised, and her next-door neighbour will take in the last-minute shopping while they're away in Germany. Dad's going to come and pick me up on Christmas Eve.'

'Any other bits and pieces? Decorations?' It was impossible for Dylan to look pointedly at Poppy's Christmas decorations because there weren't any, so he'd just have to say it.

'I meant to get a tree last weekend, but things caught up on me a bit. I'll give it a miss this year, I think, and have a really great one for next year.' She turned her mouth down in an expression of regret, which was quickly replaced with a smile. 'Baby's first Christmas tree, eh?'

The baby was going to be well provided for, if his nephew's first Christmas was anything to go by. Right now, Dylan was more concerned with *this* Christmas and with Poppy. But he sensed he was approaching Poppy's hard limits in terms of daily offers of help, and that he should leave her in peace and go to the supermarket. Tomorrow might be another matter, but he'd meet that challenge when it came…

From the antiseptic scent that had pervaded the kitchen when he'd left yesterday afternoon, Dylan had done some surreptitious cleaning. Poppy resisted the temptation to text him to remind him that they hadn't yet negotiated any rights concerning household chores, because she appreciated the gesture. And there was something about sparkling clean appliances, a full fridge, and the thought that Vera was on their side, which allowed her to relax for the evening.

And then, late on Sunday morning, her phone had rung. Dylan had said he was in the area, and asked whether he might pop in. Poppy had gulped down the quiver of excitement at the thought of seeing him again, replied in the affirmative, and then Dylan had ended the call. Clearly his approach to the telephone was much the same as his attitude to email, and he had nothing more to say.

'Any ideas what he might be up to now?' Poppy wasn't really expecting an answer. If she didn't know, she doubted her baby girl would. Maybe she should tidy up a bit, but standing up just to put the TV remote away seemed too much effort for too little reward. She was at least up and dressed, and had finished breakfast, and that was going to have to do.

The doorbell rang. His definition of *in the area* was clearly parked outside in the street. Poppy heard Dylan's voice on the intercom and buzzed him in.

He was a long time making his way upstairs. Poppy opened her front door, looking out, and saw the lift doors open.

'Dylan!' He was wearing a bright grin and holding a Christmas tree, tied up in netting.

Poppy felt her heart lurch. The effort of manoeuvring a large tree out of a small lift without scratching the wooden panelling emphasised his strong body and although his intention was clearly that the tree would promote delight, she only had eyes for him.

'Stand back,' he instructed unnecessarily. 'Don't try lifting it.'

Poppy rolled her eyes. Independence was one thing, but carrying Christmas trees quite another. Dylan strode back to the lift, where he'd left a large bag, and just as he picked it up the doors closed on him. Poppy watched as the indicator lights showed the lift travelling steadily down to the ground floor and then pausing before it made its way back up to the fifth.

'Did someone call it?' she asked as he emerged.

'There was no one there…' He put the bag inside her front door and then came back to where Poppy was standing by the tree.

'That lift looks really good, but it has a mind of its own.' Poppy shrugged.

'Suits you down to the ground, then.' Dylan picked up the tree and Poppy stood back as he manoeuvred it along the hallway.

'I'll take that as a compliment,' she called after him. A very nice compliment, because right now she felt heavy and awkward and the idea of looking good was the last thing that occurred to her.

'That's just as it was intended.' He got the tree through her front door and laid it down in the hall. Poppy followed him, shutting her front door behind them, the feeling of excitement that was rising in her chest not entirely focused on Christmas decorations.

Now that he wasn't fighting to get a large bag and a Christmas tree under control, Dylan was suddenly still and uncertain. Maybe he had his doubts about this.

'Do you mind? I can take it away if you don't want it...'

'Don't you dare, Dylan!' Poppy put herself between him and the tree. 'You'll have to go through me first before you lay one finger on this tree.'

He laughed, his face brightening. 'You like it?'

'No, I don't like it. I love it, and it was a really kind thought.'

'Good.' He turned away quickly, as if to disguise his reaction. 'Where do you want it to go?'

Poppy chose a spot in between the living and dining area, by the window. Dylan opened the bag, drawing out a tree stand, and fixed it securely in place, and then removed the netting. It was a great tree, a little bigger than the ones she'd had before, and she wondered whether her lights would stretch far enough to reach the top, but Dylan had thought of that as well. He had a box of lights in the bag along with some extra baubles, glass and gold, which would match anything. He fetched her box of decorations from the walk-in cupboard in the hall, and Poppy laid them all out on the dining table in order.

'Your decorations are lovely. Each one has a memory?'

It didn't sound like a casual enquiry, and Poppy chose her words carefully. 'These were the ones I bought for my first tree.' She pointed to a set of glass icicles. 'I seem to break one of them every year, but it doesn't matter since I started off with quite a lot of them. The wooden ones are from the Christmas market close to where my sister lives in Cologne, I got them the first year she moved out there. My mum made the fairy for me.'

'She's great.' Dylan picked up the porcelain-faced fairy, dressed in white satin with sequinned netting. 'A very special lady.'

There was no point in pretending there was nothing of Nate here. 'I bought these for the first Christmas after I was married. I was trying for a more sophisticated feel to the tree.' She laid her fingers on the sparkling white snowballs.

'They should have pride of place,' Dylan murmured.

'There's room for everything, these will be beautiful with the lights.' Poppy reached for

one of the glass baubles that Dylan had brought.
'They're the ones that I'll have on my pregnancy
Christmas tree.'

He smiled, clearly happy with the idea. 'I'll put
the lights on, shall I? Then you can hang some
of the decorations, if you want.'

'Without mince pies and hot chocolate? Dylan,
whatever are you thinking?' He'd added a box of
mince pies to her shopping list yesterday.

He chuckled. 'Okay. You can heat the mince
pies while I make a start on the lights...'

It took two hours to decorate the tree. Poppy
spent a good deal of that time on the sofa while
Dylan dealt with the top and bottom branches,
but she insisted on helping with the middle ones
that she could reach easily. Finally, Dylan carefully secured the fairy, moving her arms so that
her wand was pointing in the direction of the
sofa, which Poppy took as a hint. He cleared the
boxes away, then reappeared from the storeroom
with the vacuum cleaner to get rid of the fallen
needles and sparkle on the carpet.

'Can you stay for something to eat? It'll be
dark soon and we can have a grand switching
on of the lights.' Poppy hoped that Dylan could
stay a little longer, she didn't want this to end.
But he'd spent a good proportion of his weekend
here and surely he had somewhere else to go.
Some*one* else to spend his evening with.

'That would be great, thank you. Unless you want to take a nap?'

'If I fall asleep you can wake me. I'm too excited to miss anything.'

The afternoon had been everything that Dylan could have wished for. He couldn't bear the idea of Poppy going without a proper tree, after all the Christmases when his mother had gone out to find fallen branches in the park and meticulously painted and arranged them before hanging baubles on them. He and Sam had always told her that it was better than a boring old Christmas tree, but they all knew that it wasn't. The bare twigs were a symbol of everything they'd lost.

But Poppy had liked her tree. She'd accepted the baubles that he'd brought, making them something special in his eyes. And she'd hung the ones that reminded her of her husband, rather than hiding them away. It was all good.

She was tired now, though, and after they'd eaten she'd gone to sit down, while Dylan stacked the dishwasher. When he came back into the lounge, she'd rolled over onto her side and was snoring gently.

Maybe he should go. Or maybe wake her up, so that she could switch the lights of her Christmas tree on. Dylan sat in the darkening room, trying to make his mind up, and then Poppy shifted sleepily on the sofa.

'Uh… Sorry. I wasn't snoring, was I?'

'Only a little. I mistook it for the sound of angels singing.' Dylan chuckled as Poppy sat up straight, shooting him an indignant look.

'Come over here. I want to wash your mouth out with soap.'

She could do whatever she liked to him, as long as she was happy.

'Later. Don't you want to switch the lights on first?'

'Oh! Yes!' She was suddenly as excited as Thomas always was at the prospect. Poppy got to her feet, walking over to the tree, and Dylan caught up the remote for the lights and followed her.

'Right, then. Three…two…one… It's *Christmas*!'

Poppy flipped the button on the remote and the tree lit up. She waved her arms and began to cheer, and he followed suit. This really was Christmas. The way it should be, with the prospect of a new life and tenuous new hope tugging at him.

'It's beautiful, Dylan. Thank you so much.' Poppy turned suddenly, her hand on his shoulder pulling him down so that she could plant a kiss on his cheek.

He was powerless to resist her. Shaking suddenly from the feel of her lips brushing his skin. Her gaze met his and an action that might easily pass between friends became something that could only be shared between lovers.

'Happy Christmas, Poppy. Who knows what next year's going to bring, eh…?' It could be anything. A thousand different sensations that he'd never allowed himself to feel before.

It was both terrifying and compelling. Because one touch of Poppy's fingers, a brief kiss, had made him feel all of the things he knew he ought to feel for a woman. So much more than he'd ever felt before. If they wanted to call it friendship then he would, for Poppy's sake. But Dylan knew exactly what friendship looked and felt like, it was something he'd always treasured. This wasn't the same.

She smiled. 'I guess we'll just have to find out, won't we. Happy Christmas, Dylan.'

He longed for her lips, but they were very dangerous territory right now. And the thought this this would be the first of many Christmases— another departure from his usual modus operandi—brought him to his senses. He reached for her hand, pressing a kiss lightly on the back of her fingers. These old-fashioned marks of regard were underrated, because it felt like everything.

And he could see that *everything* in her eyes.

Her face, streaked with light from the tree, tilted up towards him. Her hand lingered in his for a few moments more than it had to, and he felt the warm pressure of her fingers sending shivers up his spine. Somehow, he knew that she was feeling that same delicious pleasure.

He drew back at almost exactly the same moment she did. This wasn't in their agreement, and Dylan knew that feeling was no excuse for doing. His head was scrambling back over the line he'd crossed, even if his heart begged for more.

'Do you have to go home and do your own decorations now?' Her smile still had the hint of that special moment, which was now beyond their grasp. And Poppy always seemed so keen not to take too much of his time for herself.

'No, mine are already done. There's a company who sneak in while you're at work and put your tree and your decorations up for you.'

Her hand flew to her mouth. 'No! That's awful!' She turned the corners of her mouth down. 'I mean…very useful for a busy person. You could have just given me their number, though.'

No, he couldn't. Being here had meant far too much to him.

'They get booked up very quickly. And just in case you were wondering… No, I don't have a date tonight either.'

He could see from the look on her face that she *had* been wondering. She turned away from him suddenly, walking back to the sofa.

'I've been thinking about…what Vera said.'

Vera had said a lot of things. Dylan knew exactly which thing Poppy meant, because he'd been thinking about it too. He'd been all in favour of the idea that Poppy should have full custody of her daughter, not just for their sakes but for his as well, and at the same time pleaded for her to allow him to be part of their lives. Vera had seen the inconsistency and now Poppy did too.

And she'd been so upfront about the way she felt, going out of her way to reassure him that their relationship could take its own course and was quite separate from the one with her husband.

'Should we talk?' Dylan couldn't help framing that as a question, even if there was no doubt in his mind. 'About…where I'm coming from in all of this?'

She nodded firmly. 'Yes. I'd like to know, Dylan.'

CHAPTER EIGHT

DYLAN HAD BEEN putting this off. He made tea for Poppy, and she went through the smiling joke of sniffing his coffee. Perhaps she knew that it was difficult to find somewhere to start.

'You have a Christmas grinch somewhere in your past?' She'd clearly decided that he needed a bit of a nudge, and Dylan smiled.

'Yeah, I guess. My father left my mother when Sam and I were eleven. He'd been having an affair with someone at his office, a divorcee with a child.'

'I guess that messed up Christmas,' Poppy prompted him gently.

'It messed up everything. My mum hadn't seen it coming and she was devastated. So sad… I didn't help her much. I started to cut school and generally act up. My father had always been a bit of a role model for me.'

'Isn't that how it should be? For an eleven-year-old boy?'

Dylan shrugged. 'Maybe. I chose the wrong

person. My father seemed like someone you could rely on, but that was only because it suited him. After he left, it was very much a matter of *out of sight, out of mind.* All his attention went to his new partner and her child.'

A tear rolled down Poppy's cheek. 'I'm so sorry, Dylan. That must have been devastating for you.'

'Much more so for my mum. She was determined to be there for me and Sam when we got home from school, but she had to get a part-time job just to make ends meet. My father had obviously been planning this for some time, he had his own business and his new partner was an employee, so there was room for some creative accounting. He paid very little child maintenance.'

Poppy shook her head. 'So you and your brother probably didn't have all that much at Christmas.'

'Not much that you need money for. Mum made the best of everything and went without herself. Things got better, Mum got a full-time job when Sam and I were older, and when we both went to university we agreed to pool what money we had and give Mum the Christmas she deserved. We got a tree and some nice presents for her, and cooked lunch. Imagine two eighteen-year-old lads in a kitchen...'

'I'm sure she loved it. However you did.'

'Actually, we didn't do too badly. We got together and planned it down to the last moment. Mum had to intervene a couple of times, but mostly we did it ourselves. Sam nearly singed his eyebrows, he was a bit too generous with the brandy on the Christmas pudding, but apart from that we had no casualties.'

Poppy chuckled, leaning forward to reach her mug and take a sip of her tea. Still waiting. She was sometimes a bit too perceptive, and she knew that this wasn't just a guided tour of his Christmases past.

'I can't commit, Poppy. I think of all the promises my father broke, all of the pain he caused, and it just terrifies me.'

She regarded him steadily. 'But from what I hear you say about your brother… What makes you think that you're like your father and not him?'

Good question.

'Sam and I are alike, we're both pretty certain about not making promises we can't keep. He knows for sure that he can keep his promises to Sophie and Thomas.'

'He's had the time to think that all through, though, hasn't he. I've had time to think through exactly what I want with this pregnancy. You really haven't.'

Dylan nodded. Maybe he'd found something in Poppy that he'd been looking for all his life, but he couldn't be sure. And his fears were bearing down on him, too heavy a weight to resist.

'You don't often find that thing that Sam and Sophie have.'

'I think I see it now. You don't want to sign up for something you think you may not be able to fulfil…' Poppy thought for a moment. 'But Thomas…?'

She'd done him the favour of listening, and responding without judgement.

Dylan smiled. 'I'm his uncle. I make a really good job of that.'

'Okay. I get it. This is somewhere for us to start from, and we can work out how we want things to be as we go. I just wanted to know that you weren't doing all of this because you felt you had to.'

'I don't. It's what I want, Poppy.'

She nodded, smiling at him. 'Well, the baby loves your Christmas tree.'

Dylan threw her a sceptical look. 'And you know that how?'

'She makes her presence felt. Sometimes she kicks and moves around and sometimes she's calm. When we switched the lights on I felt her almost dancing with excitement.'

Just the way Poppy had been. He wanted so much to ask—to lay his hand on her stomach and feel the baby kick. But that seemed a step too far.

Then Poppy reached out, taking his hand. 'You want to feel her?'

'Do you really have to ask?'

She shook her head, laughing. Poppy put his hand onto her stomach and he felt nothing. No movement. He wondered whether he should take his hand away, lifting it slightly.

'No, stay there. But more pressure.' Poppy clasped her hands over his, pushing a little. Then he felt it.

'Whoa! Does she do that all the time?'

'No, that was a big one. I think she's settling down again. Maybe she knows it's you.'

The idea hovered in the air, shining and magical. And then Dylan tore it down, unable to contemplate it. 'She feels someone.'

'She can hear voices—she's been able to hear mine for ages now. And yours is lower, she responds differently.' Poppy gave him a searching look. 'Before I was pregnant, I knew all about babies because I'm a doctor. I've learned a great deal more since.'

Dylan nodded. As long as Poppy allowed him to keep his hand right there and feel his daughter kick, he didn't much care whether the baby knew it was him or not. Just that she knew it was someone who loved her.

'Do you have a name for her yet?'

'I did think of a few when I first knew it was a girl. I couldn't work out which might suit her best, and thought I'd make up my mind when I got the chance to meet her face to face.'

'Good idea.' Maybe he'd get the chance to be there when Poppy did that. Be one of the first to call the baby by name. That was unlikely. By the time the baby was born, Poppy's family would be back in England and they'd be the ones to witness those first momentous decisions.

There was something more he could do, though. If Poppy took pleasure in it, then maybe their baby girl would feel that. He took his hand from her stomach, bidding a silent *See you later* to his daughter.

'I saw a box of other decorations in your hall cupboard. Tinsel and greenery. Were you thinking of using them this year?'

Poppy laughed. 'I'd come to the conclusion I wouldn't be using any of it. I usually put those around the fireplace.'

'I could… You could tell me where you want everything…' Dylan shrugged, leaving the offer as open as he could so that Poppy could say no if she wanted to.

'Yes, Dylan, thank you! That would be wonderful...'

Sleeping well wasn't really an option these days, but Poppy had gone to bed early and, apart from the now regular trips to the bathroom, she'd stayed there for some time. All the same, just getting to work was an increasing effort, even if her first glimpse of the decorations in the sitting room buoyed her.

There was an oat and banana muffin hidden away behind her printer. It got her through three pre-op consultations, carefully explaining to each patient what to expect, and checking on their condition. Then the fourth...

Mrs Wise had wobbled into the hospital with the aid of her walking stick, and someone had taken the precaution of putting her into a wheelchair. She had a relatively small meningioma, and its position didn't account for her unsteady gait. Poppy could see in the notes that Dylan had referred her to Orthopaedics but, as far as she knew, ancient Tyrolean walking sticks weren't standard issue.

'I see that Mr Harper referred you down to Orthopaedics.' Poppy peered at the screen in front of her. 'For your knee?'

'Yes, that's right. When you get to my age you always seem to have more than one thing at a time. They're going to keep an eye on it.'

'Okay. It says here they've given you some exercises to do.' Poppy was mentally measuring the distance between the desk and the couch, and wondering how she was going to carry out an examination without one of them falling on the floor.

'Yes, dear. I do them every day. Are you looking forward to the baby?'

'Yes.' Poppy decided not to elaborate. It was Mrs Wise's condition that they were supposed to be discussing.

'Is it your first? My Keith was a difficult birth, you know…'

Poppy didn't much want to hear it. Childbirth stories from forty years ago weren't her favourite subject at the moment. 'I'm fine, Mrs Wise, thank you. This appointment is for us to discuss how *you* are…'

Mrs Wise leaned forward. 'Boy or girl?'

Enough! Reaching for her phone might be an unwelcome sign that she couldn't cope. Right now, Poppy didn't care because examining Mrs Wise was going to involve an obvious breach of Health and Safety guidelines.

'Just a moment, Mrs Wise.' She couldn't help

a sigh of relief as Dylan answered his phone. 'Mr Harper, do you have ten minutes, please?'

There was a short pause as Dylan assessed the situation. Then, 'Yep. What's up?'

'Mrs Wise is here. Since you're the surgeon who'll be carrying out her meningioma procedure next week, I wondered if you might like to pop up and see her.' Poppy added as much information as she could.

'On my way...'

Poppy managed to steer Mrs Wise away from any potential medical issues surrounding the birth, and stuck with telling her that she didn't have a name for her baby girl just yet. Then a knock sounded on the door, and Dylan appeared. His eyes travelled from the wheelchair to the examination couch, and he gave a small nod.

'Mrs Wise.' He sat down in the chair next to her. 'Remember me? I'm Dylan Harper and I saw you last time you were here. I'll be carrying out your procedure next week.'

'I remember. Hello, Doctor.' Mrs Wise smiled politely. At least she wasn't calling Dylan *dear*. Poppy turned her computer screen towards him so that he could see it.

'I referred you down to Orthopaedics, didn't I? Have you seen anyone there yet?'

'Yes, they were very good. Very nice. I have exercises.' Mrs Wise beamed at Dylan.

'And they gave you a walking frame?' That wasn't a particularly inspired guess, it would have been an obvious move.

'Yes, but I left it at home. I prefer my stick.'

Dylan regarded the stick with interest. 'It's a nice one. Where did you get it?'

'My late husband brought it home from a walking holiday when he was eighteen. We used to walk everywhere together, you know, and he always took his stick.'

Poppy could identify with that. She'd used Nate's things, worn his sweaters at first, just for the comfort they'd brought. Then she'd made a resolution and gone through everything, saving some things as mementos and giving the rest to the charity shop.

'I understand.' Dylan looked up at her when she spoke, his blue eyes suddenly thoughtful. 'It's a very precious thing, isn't it.'

'Yes, Doctor.'

'Then I think you should keep it at home, where it won't be lost or broken, and you'll always have it to remember him by. The walking frame is just something to help you, it doesn't matter if it gets damaged.'

Mrs Wise thought for a moment. 'Yes, I think you're right. I'll do that.'

'That's great.' Dylan shot a smile in Poppy's direction and then turned his attention to Mrs

Wise. 'Now, I'll just help you over to the examination couch and check you over to make sure everything's as it should be before your operation. Then you can go home, and I'll see you next week.'

'Yes, Doctor. Thank you.'

Dylan was perfect. Smiling and authoritative, with a trace of mischief in his blue eyes that seemed to indicate he was on his patient's side as he checked her reflexes and reviewed her scans. Anyone would fall for him. He helped her down from the couch, installing her safely back in the wheelchair.

'Right, then. Everything's as it should be, Mrs Wise. I think we'll organise some hospital transport to get you home, shall we? Unless that's already sorted out.'

Mrs Wise shook her head. 'I came on the bus. I didn't want to be any trouble.'

Somehow, Dylan managed not to roll his eyes. 'It's no trouble. Making sure you get home safely is one of the things we're here for. I'll just wheel you out and speak to the receptionist, and she'll look after you.'

Mrs Wise gave Poppy a cheery wave, wishing her all the luck in the world with the baby, and Poppy grinned at her, telling she didn't need any luck for her operation next week because Mr Harper was the best surgeon in the department.

She caught a flash of Dylan's blue-eyed smile before he turned, manoeuvring the wheelchair through the door.

'Thanks, Dylan. Was that your lunch break, or can I buy you lunch?' Poppy was feeling a little annoyed with herself that she'd had to call him for help, even if it had been the obvious right thing to do.

'I've only got fifteen minutes. You can buy me lunch tomorrow if you like.' He sat down in the chair on the other side of her desk, clearly willing to spend that valuable time with her.

'I'm seeing a new side of you. Charming all your patients…' Poppy shifted in her seat, trying to get comfortable again.

'Really?' He flashed her an amused look. 'Are you suggesting that I switch on the charm to get what I want?'

'Face it, Dylan. You can be charming and you wanted to get through to her for her own good. I'm just seeing a different side of you now, one that doesn't get much of an airing at meetings and in the operating theatre.'

'Ah. That's all right then. I'd hate to think that it was my principal contribution to the department.' He was teasing, but there was a wry edge to his humour. Poppy had heard the way the nurses talked about him, and she'd be annoyed if any of the male members of staff said those things about her.

'I've always respected you as a fine surgeon. Now that I've got to know you out of work, I appreciate your charm. Getting through to people is a thing as well.'

His lips twitched as if he was trying not to make too much of the compliment. 'Thank you.'

'You're welcome.' Poppy decided to change the subject. 'I'm going to have to slow down a bit, aren't I? Not being able to operate until after the baby's born is one thing, but if I need to call someone in to help with consultations then I'm becoming a liability.'

'Liability's a bit harsh. But you're less than three weeks from your due date, and maybe it's time to think about spending some time at home.' He smiled suddenly. 'Ideally, of course, you'd go into labour around lunchtime, have the baby and then be back at work the following morning.'

Poppy chuckled. 'You know that's not going to happen, don't you? I'm really looking forward to my maternity leave, and spending some time with our little girl.'

Slip of the tongue. Poppy had caught herself thinking of her baby as Dylan's child too, and the idea had escaped into the open air now.

If he heard it, he said nothing. That was good,

because Poppy didn't entirely know how she felt about it.

'I'm looking forward to seeing her.' His gaze was scanning her face, looking for a reaction.

'You can come and see her any time you like.' Poppy had told him that often enough, but Dylan always seemed to want to hear it one more time. 'You can bring whatever you like as well. Supplies from the supermarket. You could bring coffee, even. For me, that is, not her...'

He chuckled. 'Aren't you supposed to stay off the coffee after she's born?'

'For the most part. I can have a cup a day, as long as it's not right before I feed her.'

'Ah. Well, you can call and demand emergency coffee any time you like. Day or night. As long as I'm not working, of course.'

'Careful what you wish for, Dylan,' Poppy teased him.

'I am.' Dylan murmured the words but there was no doubt in her mind that he meant them. It was hard thinking of him as the man she might rely on, but when she looked into his clear blue eyes it became frighteningly easy.

He looked at his watch. 'I've got to go. I've got a surgery scheduled. If I leave my charm behind on your desk, would you look after it?'

Poppy chuckled. 'Of course. I'll give it a saucer of milk and lock the door in case it escapes.'

He laughed, making his way to the door. 'Get something to eat. Sounds as if your blood sugar's beginning to drop.'

Dylan closed the door behind him, and suddenly the room felt darker. Poppy wriggled in her seat, trying to get comfortable, and then decided to get up and walk a little. Pacing seemed like a good idea right now.

Spending more time at home would be hard. She'd miss her morning muffins—she could hardly expect Dylan to deliver them to her flat. And she'd miss the reassurance of seeing him every day, even if it was just a fleeting glimpse of his smile, or catching sight of him at the far end of a corridor. Letting herself flirt with him from time to time.

But then, when she got back home she'd see the photograph of her and Nate's wedding, sitting next to the plant he'd come home with the day before he'd died, which Poppy had nurtured so carefully in the weeks and months after she'd lost him. And she'd feel guilty about wanting to be with Dylan because she and Nate had been so happy, made so many promises, only a few of which they'd had time to keep.

Poppy knew what Nate would say about that. They'd talked about it once, feeling safe in the knowledge that all their what-ifs were never going to happen. Nate would want her to move on and live her life. But she'd disagreed with him then, and it seemed wrong not to afford him the respect of disagreeing with him now.

Moving on and living your life was a lot easier to say than it was to do… But the baby was moving on and so was her body. Dylan's suggestion that she slowed down was a good one, and it was time she listened to it.

CHAPTER NINE

DYLAN HAD TEXTED HER, saying he couldn't make lunch on Tuesday, and so Poppy had conceded to the inevitable and gone to see the head of Neurology instead. He'd suggested that she confine herself to seeing patients in the morning and go home in the early afternoon for the rest of the week, and since she'd be taking time off over Christmas anyway it made sense for her to start her maternity leave officially next week. The department would miss her but they'd cope and he already had a replacement lined up, who would be able to cover Christmas and the New Year.

It was sooner than she'd expected, but Poppy could see the sense in it. Someone who was able to take on her usual workload would make staffing over the holidays much easier, and she'd started to feel the strain of needing to be at work every day. Poppy had reluctantly agreed to the plan.

She'd texted Dylan to tell him, and he'd sent back a smile. Clearly, he was busy, and she shouldn't be needy when he had patients to attend to. And, for this week at least, she still had morning muffins, a different flavour every time. On Friday there had been a note attached to the bag, saying that he could leave work a little early to take her home, if she would wait for him, and Poppy had texted back to thank him. Several heavy hints from Maisie at Reception had told her that there would be goodbyes to say at lunchtime, and she could spend the rest of the afternoon packing up her personal belongings.

There had been cake, and a whip-round had afforded presents for both Poppy and the baby. Poppy had cried when she'd read the messages in the large card, and spent the next two hours thanking everyone, as people dropped in and then left again to go back to work.

At three o'clock, Maisie had taken care of the paper plates and cups and the empty soft drinks bottles and her office was spick and span again, apart from some chocolate cake which had been trodden into the carpet. Poppy was sitting with her feet up on the empty box that she was supposed to be taking her personal belongings home in when a knock sounded on the door and Kate burst in.

'Sorreee…! Sorry I missed your party, honey.'

Poppy smiled. 'I know you would have made it if you could. Busy down in A&E?'

'Frantic. But I've got fifteen minutes to myself now, and I came up to see if you were still here.'

'You haven't got rid of me quite yet. Dylan's operating today, but he's going to take me home afterwards in the car.' Poppy tapped the box with her foot. 'I've still got to pack my things up. Do you want some cake? I saved you some.'

'You star. Yes, please. I haven't had anything since breakfast.'

'Have some of my tea, I don't really want it.' Poppy pushed the freshly made cup of herbal tea across her desk and took a large foil-wrapped slice of cake from her desk drawer.

'Mmm. Thanks.' Kate unwrapped the cake, beaming at it. 'You've been seeing a bit of Dylan lately.'

'Yes. I should tell you…'

Kate held up her hand. 'You don't need to ex- plain. I don't listen to gossip and it's your busi- ness.'

Poppy wanted to tell someone, and Kate was her closest friend. 'It's okay. I want you to know. There was a mix-up at the fertility clinic. Dylan's the father of my baby.'

Kate lost interest in the cake, staring at her open-mouthed. 'It's true, then. What's Dylan doing donating sperm? He's already seduced half the hospital.'

'Not *half*…' Poppy turned the corners of her

mouth down, regretting that this had been one of her first thoughts, too.

'Okay. A good proportion of the single women under thirty-five. And it's a big place.'

'He had his reasons, Kate.' Poppy didn't feel comfortable talking about Dylan's nephew. 'And this wasn't his fault any more than it's mine—he's been really good about it. I have full custody and responsibility for my baby, just as I wanted, and he's…he says he'd like to help out. As a friend. He'll be her uncle, just as you're going to be her Auntie Kate.'

'Hmm. Sounds cosy.' Kate took a sip of tea, looking at Poppy thoughtfully.

'Give him a chance.' Poppy frowned at her friend. It wasn't like Kate to be so negative about people. 'He's been there for me. He leaves breakfast muffins in my office every morning.'

Kate nodded. Poppy knew that would impress her. 'Where from?'

'Don't worry, they're not all fats and sugar—he gets most of them from the health food restaurant.'

'Hmm. Better than a *Thinking of you* text, I suppose. You do know he's seeing someone?'

Of course Dylan was seeing someone. By all accounts, he was rarely without a partner, however uncommitted those relationships were. It didn't mean anything. Dylan had told her how he felt about commitment. That didn't mean he couldn't love their baby when she was born.

'Yes, I know. I told you, Kate, we're friends. I don't want anyone else, not after Nate.'

Kate turned the corners of her mouth down. 'You and Nate were special. Just as long as Dylan respects that, and he's being straight with you. Not stringing you along with muffins and promises. The ones from the health food place are enough to turn anyone's head.'

'It's okay, really. We've sorted everything out between us, and Dylan's done a lot to make sure that everything's the way I wanted it. Who's he seeing?' The question slipped out.

'So you *didn't* know…?'

'I knew. I don't know who.'

'Jeannie from Orthopaedics. I saw them in the canteen together, very wrapped up in whatever they were saying. I happened to walk out behind them…' Kate shrugged as Poppy raised her eyebrows. 'I did really just happen to finish at the same time they did. Dylan had his arm around her as they got into the lift and, just as the doors closed, I saw them hug each other. It wasn't a friendly hug either.'

'You were taking notes?'

'No, of course not. Don't be obtuse, Poppy. We all know the difference between a *See you later* hug and a *See you later between the sheets* one.'

'When was this?'

'Tuesday. I thought you said you knew?'

'I did. In general terms.' Although Tuesday… That felt a bit like a slap in the face because Dylan had cancelled lunch with Poppy to meet Jeannie.

And Poppy *knew* Jeannie, she wasn't just an anonymous name. Tall and willowy, with long dark hair… Poppy didn't want to think about her blue eyes, or that Dylan might find them just as mesmerising as his own were. Or her easy-going nature, which had to be a relief after all that she and Dylan had been through recently.

Time for a change of subject. Poppy had been quite clear that she didn't want to get in the way of Dylan's love life, and she needed to swallow down whatever she felt now and stick to the plan. She didn't want Kate to think badly of him either, they might be bumping into each other at her place after the baby was born.

'It's not a problem, Kate. I'm more interested in you and Jon. How are things going?'

'Good. Really good, actually. You were right— the problems we've been having aren't because there's anything basically wrong, it's just that we never get to see each other with Jon working nights. He's on days again now for the next five weeks and he's going to ask about making that permanent.'

Poppy nodded. 'They're sure to agree. Jon's a really valuable member of staff and they won't risk losing him. He just needs to be a bit less accommodating about what everyone else wants.'

'Yeah.' Kate's fingers strayed to her engagement ring. 'When I got home last night there was a trail of rose petals leading upstairs and he was running me a hot bath. And we're spending the weekend at a hotel in Hampshire, it's a really nice place.'

'Fantastic. Where did Jon get rose petals from at this time of year?'

Kate rolled her eyes. 'Trust me, honey, that was the last thing on my mind at the time...'

It had been a long week. Dylan had been busy and he'd missed Poppy's goodbye party, but he made it up to her office at four o'clock, after spending six hours in the operating theatre.

'How did it go?' Poppy was reclining in her office chair and gave him a smile.

'Well.' The surgery had taken longer than he'd anticipated, but he was pleased with the results. 'I've spoken with the relatives—are you okay to stay another half hour while I check on the patient in Recovery?'

'As long as you like. I've boxed up all my stuff now, and it'll take me a good half hour to make a quick tour of the department and say goodbye to everyone.' She produced a bottle of water from her empty desk drawer, smiling up at him. 'Sit down for a moment, you look tired.'

He didn't feel tired, but that would hit him later on, probably after he got Poppy back to her flat and settled in. But she knew that he'd be thirsty and he sat down, taking the bottle gratefully.

'I saved you some cake as well. I had such a beautiful card, and such thoughtful gifts.'

Water first. Dylan took a long swig from the bottle, nodding to indicate that was just what he needed. Then he looked inside one of the gift bags on Poppy's desk. There were things for the baby, some sleepsuits in various sizes and a warm quilted snowsuit.

'This is very cute.' He pulled the snowsuit out of the bag, examining the three penguins embroidered on the front.

'Isn't it. And look, they got something for me, too. It's my favourite scent.' Poppy's tone was a little flat, her smile not as glowing as usual. Maybe she was just tired, and needed to get home after what must have been an emotional day for her.

But she pushed the second gift bag across the desk towards him and Dylan looked at the bottles inside. Body lotion, hand cream and scent, an expensive brand. Poppy was gorgeous just as she was, but this gift was a little luxury, designed to make her feel that way. He wished he'd thought of it.

'It's lovely.' Dylan thought he saw tears in her eyes when he looked up but she dabbed them away quickly. Today had been more taxing for Poppy than he'd thought. 'I'm sorry I couldn't be there for your party.'

'It's okay. We're not joined at the hip. We have our own lives.'

Maybe Poppy had been having doubts. They'd seemed so close last weekend, and Dylan couldn't deny that it had given him pause for thought. He would never abandon his child, he was sure of that, but he needed also to think about a sustainable relationship with Poppy. He'd been so careful with words, never promising anything he wasn't sure he could deliver, but maybe he needed to be a little more careful with his actions.

'I can take your box down to the car and we can meet outside. Whatever you're more comfortable with.'

'You're giving me a lift home, Dylan. People can think whatever they like.' Poppy thought for a moment. 'It's up to you, though. You're going to be the one staying here and facing the music.'

A swell of warmth suddenly burst in his chest. There would be plenty of time to work out their boundaries later. If Poppy needed, or even just wanted, his support today then he'd be proud to give it. 'There's nothing to face. Let's waltz out of here together.'

Finally, she smiled. A *real* smile, not just the pale glimmer that had been playing around her lips. 'Very smooth. Am I going to have to deal with your charming side all the time, now that we're not officially working together?'

'Yep.' He grinned back at her. They were both tired, that was all. 'I'll be back in half an hour. Don't eat my cake.'

Three-quarters of an hour later, he pulled out of the hospital's underground car park, into the dark streets. Just for the hell of it he took a detour along Regent Street so that Poppy could enjoy the Christmas lights, and then headed north to her flat.

She walked ahead of him up the steps to her building, as if she couldn't wait to get home. Her life was entering a new phase, and somehow her eagerness to meet it allayed his own fears about the changes ahead. He hurried to open the main door for her, and she walked towards the lift.

'Oh!' Poppy stopped suddenly. Yellow and black striped tape was secured across the lift doors, and there was a laminated notice taped to them.

'Five days!' He glanced at the notice, reading it quickly. 'Since when does it take five days to mend a lift?'

'It's an old lift. They have to use a specialist company.' Poppy shot him a dismayed look. As well she might, because there were six floors of steps between her and her home.

'Come back to mine. We'll go from there.'

Poppy stiffened with disapproval. 'No, I can make it up there. If you help me.'

'And then you'll have to make it all the way down again to get back out. It's fifteen minutes to my place, and we can sit down and decide what to do.'

'But… No, Dylan. I need my things.'

'We can come back tomorrow for anything you need.' Dylan was happy to give way to Poppy on most things, but not this. 'If you won't come to my flat, then I'll take you somewhere else.'

'But I have a perfectly comfortable flat, which has everything I need. It's just a few stairs. You could help me up them, couldn't you?' Poppy shot him an imploring look which almost broke his resolve.

'Yes, I could, but I'm not going to. I wouldn't be doing you any favours.'

'Dylan…!' Poppy pressed her lips together, nodding at a couple who were just entering the lobby. 'The lift's out.'

'Not again.' The woman grimaced. 'Are you going to be all right…?'

'Thanks, but we'll be fine. We're going to my place.' Dylan spoke before Poppy had a chance to, and was aware of her frowning at him. The woman nodded, and made for the stairs with her companion.

'So you're turning down offers of help on my behalf, now?' Poppy practically hissed the words at him.

'Do you know her?' Dylan asked, ignoring her glare.

'Only to say hello to. But they live on the third floor and I expect they wouldn't mind my sitting down for a while to get my breath back, before I tackle the rest of the stairs.'

'I'm not worried about you getting out of breath, I'm worried that you'll fall. And you're just making things unnecessarily difficult. If there's a friend you'd prefer to stay with then I'll take you there. What about Kate?' If Poppy refused to stay with him, Dylan would just have to accept it, but he wouldn't leave her to depend on the help of virtual strangers.

Poppy puffed out a breath. 'Kate and Jon, her fiancé, have been going through a rocky patch. They've been making time for one date night a week and they're going away this weekend. My turning up at short notice is hardly going to put them in the mood for scattering rose petals.'

Probably not, although that was what friends were for. But at least Poppy was beginning to realise that she couldn't stay here.

'Family?'

'I'd usually go to Mum and Dad's or to my sister's, but they're in Germany at the moment.'

'Right then. Since I'm still in the country, and not having any relationship problems, it sounds as if you're stuck with me. Is that really so bad?'

Suddenly her defences dropped. 'No, it's really nice of you. I'm sorry I just…panicked for a moment. Home's always the place you feel safest.'

And it was where Poppy had lived with her husband. Dylan understood that, and didn't underestimate her need to feel its comfort right now.

'There's nothing to be sorry for. It's just for tonight and we can weigh up the options in the morning. If you give me your keys then I'll go and fetch whatever you need.'

She opened her bag and handed her keys over. 'I've got my hospital bag already packed, that has everything I'll need for a night, and it's in the hall. Would you bring my V-shaped pillow, please, it's on my bed. And there's another memory foam pillow as well.'

'Okay. You go and sit in the car while I take on the stairs. Give me a call if anything else comes to mind…'

CHAPTER TEN

POPPY WAS FEELING a little ashamed of herself.
She'd hoped that Dylan might take her home and
then find an excuse to leave, because jealousy
was one of those emotions that was better handled alone. But she knew that staying here was a
really bad idea, and she was just going to have to
make the best of things. She obediently went to
sit in his car, and when she saw the lights in her
flat come on she called Dylan with a few more
things to add to the list.

She heard the tension in his voice lighten, and
several minutes after the windows on the top
floor of the block darkened he walked back towards the car. Leaning in, he put the fairy from
the tree into her hand.

'I thought she might like to come too.'

Poppy smiled at him, trying not to cry. Dylan
seemed to take her weepiness in his stride, but
she was starting to become impatient with it. She
really wanted her mum at the moment, and the
fairy was just perfect.

'I brought some of your tea as well.' He grinned and Poppy laughed, wrinkling her nose.

'I just can't get away from the tea, can I? I was hoping that we might call this an emergency and have to drink coffee.'

Dylan chuckled. 'I'm afraid it's not that much of an emergency...'

His flat was in a large, solidly built block. There were two lifts, and when he pressed the call button the doors of one slid open. They rode smoothly up to the penthouse, and Dylan ushered her through a small lobby to his front door.

It looked as if his was the only apartment on the top floor of the building, set back a little from the façade of the lower floors. The double-height windows at the front gave a marvellous view of the lights of London, and at the back steps led up from the huge living area to a deep gallery, which appeared to be Dylan's private space. Poppy looked around, wondering where she was going to sleep, and he smiled, walking to a door that led to a covered space under the gallery.

'This is the spare bedroom.' He leaned into the room, depositing her case by the door, as if she'd already taken up residence there and it was out of bounds for him. When Poppy looked inside she saw a cosy room which boasted a large double bed.

'The bathroom's next door—' he indicated

another, closed, door '—and the kitchen's just around the corner from there.'

The three rooms, bedroom, bathroom and the open-plan kitchen, were all tucked neatly under the gallery. Dylan's bedroom space must be almost as large as the seating area downstairs, and when Poppy looked upwards she saw the top of bookshelves at one side. He must have an office up there, too.

The Christmas decorators had done a good job. There was a large tree, standing by the full height glazing in the living space, garlands threaded along the top of the steel and glass barriers that bordered the gallery, and shimmering clusters of tinsel and baubles by the windows. Poppy clutched her mother's fairy protectively to her chest.

'Not quite as Christmassy as yours...' He smiled, nodding towards the fairy. He was right, the fairy might not have so much shine but she was one of a kind. These decorations were beautiful but they were the sort of thing you might find adorning any public space at this time of the year.

'It's lovely, Dylan.'

He nodded, turning away. Dylan was nothing if not perceptive, and he must know the difference between a gorgeous piece of architecture and a home. 'Make yourself comfortable. Would you like some tea?'

'Thank you. That would be great.' Poppy walked across to the seating area, where a large sofa and several chairs were placed around a glass-topped coffee table. Almost defiantly, she draped her coat untidily across the back of an armchair, although she was sure there must be a concealed cupboard for it somewhere, and sat down, putting the fairy down on the coffee table in front of her. At least the two of them were in this together.

He reappeared, carrying two cups of tea, and sat down in a chair opposite her. They sat for a moment in silence as Poppy tried to think of something to say. Preferably something that didn't have anything to do with Jeannie.

'You have a lovely view here. There must always be something different.'

He nodded. 'Yeah, I like it.'

'I'll be okay on my own, if you have plans…' Maybe the plans involved staying in rather than going out. Poppy would just have to hope that Dylan would go to Jeannie's place, since the open-plan gallery would make it difficult to ignore a second guest for the night.

'No plans.' He shifted in his seat suddenly, leaning forward to reach for his tea. 'You must be hungry. I'll make some dinner.'

'Don't go to any trouble. Have you got any bread? Maybe peanut butter?'

He chuckled. 'You call peanut butter sandwiches dinner? I was going to do shepherd's pie with lentils and plenty of vegetables. I've got some ice cream in the freezer.'

Dylan's menu choice sounded surprisingly homely. And delicious. Her stomach began to growl appreciatively before she had a chance to tell him that he shouldn't go to any trouble. Dylan grinned and got to his feet.

'I'll take that as a yes. Sit tight, it'll be thirty-five minutes.'

Dylan sat alone, staring out at the lights of London. They were usually calming, the world going by beneath him something that he could lose himself in. Tonight, his thoughts were in overdrive and difficult to ignore.

Poppy had been quiet all evening. Probably tired—today had been a busy day for her, and one that marked a big change in her life. It was her defensiveness that bothered him, because Dylan had thought they'd set that aside and reached an understanding.

It was still fragile, though. He'd stepped back a little this week, telling himself that Poppy needed to find her own space. But maybe he was the one who needed to find some space.

They ate in the kitchen, because that seemed rather more homely than the large table out in the main living space. Poppy helped him stack the dishwasher and then curled up on the sofa, obviously exhausted, and she'd agreed readily when Dylan suggested she might like to watch some TV in bed. He unlocked the door between the bathroom and the spare room, telling her he'd use the shower room upstairs, and then drew the curtains and found the remote for the TV. Poppy picked up her Christmas tree fairy, bidding him a smiling goodnight.

Now that the fairy was gone, the remaining Christmas decorations seemed somehow cold and lifeless. Dylan climbed the steps to the gallery, kicking off his shoes and flinging himself down onto the bed. This evening had handed him just the opportunity he'd wanted, hadn't it? An emergency, which hadn't hurt anyone, but had given him the chance to come to the rescue and show Poppy that she could rely on him. But it tasted bitter. Poppy really hadn't wanted to come here, and Dylan was having his doubts about how they'd manage, living together for five days. They'd both had their reasons for deciding to live alone, and this was a sea-change that had maybe come a little too soon.

Poppy's warmth, her sharp but forgiving tongue and her creative approach to life might be challenging, but Dylan had a feeling that it might just save him. Tomorrow might turn into a mess of conflicting emotions and uncertainties, his and hers. But he could deal with that far better than he could deal with the distance which seemed to have opened up between them this evening.

Poppy had watched a little TV and slept for a while. But keeping herself confined to the spare room and the adjoining bathroom had provided the rest that she so badly needed. She knew what she had to do now. It was okay for Dylan to be involved with the baby, but they both had their own lives.

She almost faltered when she found that he'd been up before her. He'd clearly been at some pains to let her sleep in, and came hurrying down the steps that led to the gallery when he heard her moving around in the kitchen. Breakfast was a process of emptying one of the kitchen cupboards to provide her with a choice of cereals, and Dylan's smile as he spun different boxes of tea in the air to encourage her to choose.

He seemed so alive. Casual clothes, jeans and a sweater suited him so well and his blond hair and blue eyes seemed brighter when they weren't combined with the greys and dark blues of the suits he wore to work. He made coffee for himself and kept her company at the kitchen table while she ate.

'I've decided...' Poppy had finished her granola mixed with yoghurt and raspberries and her spoon clattered into the empty bowl. 'It's really good of you to put me up here, but I'd like to go to a hotel until my lift's back in action.'

His gaze darkened suddenly. 'A hotel?'

She'd missed this too. Someone to call her out on her decisions. People had gingerly offered advice after Nate had died, but the common thread had always been that she should do whatever felt right and that there were no rules. Dylan was different, and he had no hesitation in telling her what he really thought.

'Yes.'

'Why?'

Poppy took a breath. 'I'll have all my meals prepared for me, I can do just as I please, and I won't be in anyone's way.'

Dylan looked around, as if searching for a point that he'd missed. 'You can do all that here, can't you? We're not exactly falling over each other.'

'Yes, but... It's really nice of you, Dylan, but you have your own life.' Poppy decided that she shouldn't make it all about him, even if his life was probably a bit more eventful than hers at the moment. 'I do, too.'

His questioning gaze seemed to bore into her. 'What's going on, Poppy? You didn't find a plague of insects under the bed, or an odd smell in the bathroom, did you?'

'No! Your guest room's lovely and so is the bathroom. I was very comfortable last night.'

'But you won't be comfortable tonight?'

'No. I'd prefer to go to a hotel.'

It was one thing to know that Dylan and Jeannie were probably spending their nights together, but actually being here and having to watch him go... That was far too much information. Poppy was trying very hard *not* to be jealous right now, and finding it much more difficult than she'd anticipated.

His brow darkened. Dylan got to his feet, grabbing her empty bowl and putting it into the sink, his movements betraying a strand of anger. Then he walked through to the main living area, clearly looking for something that needed to be tidied away and finding nothing. Poppy took her phone from her pocket, scrolling through the list of hotels she'd found at two o'clock this morning, before falling asleep again. If Dylan was going to sulk... Fair enough, he'd get over it and she'd just get on and do what she'd decided already.

Then he marched back into the kitchen, leaning against the counter, as if coming any closer might bring her within the radius of an angry emotion that he didn't want to share.

'What?' Poppy glared at him. She might be pregnant but she was quite capable of arguing with him if she wanted to.

Dylan folded his arms, thinking for a moment. She wished he wouldn't do that—he could say what he thought without censoring anything that might be too blunt.

'You obviously have something on your mind, Poppy, and I'd be grateful if you'd just say it. If you just don't want to be around me, then say so. I might not like it very much, but it strikes me that being honest with each other is the only way that we can make our arrangement work.'

Honest. That worked two ways.

'I know you're seeing someone, Dylan. Clearly, my presence here is cramping your style...' Maybe that was a bit *too* honest.

'What?' He looked genuinely puzzled. 'You think I have the time to see anyone right now? Or the inclination?'

'I have no idea what your inclinations are, Dylan. I just think that respecting each other's space and that we have different lives is a good way to move forward.' That sounded a bit more constructive.

He spread his hands in a gesture of frustration. 'I agree, Poppy. If either of us is seeing anyone, then it's probably a good idea to mention it. It's okay to mention it, because we're friends and we both want to do the best thing for the baby. But I'm not. Are you?'

Poppy rolled her eyes. 'Of course not.'

'So what makes you think I am?'

She didn't want to bring Kate into this, but light was already dawning on Dylan's face. 'Kate told you, didn't she. That she'd seen me and Jeannie in the canteen together. I noticed her staring at me and then looking away.'

'She saw you on the way to the lift as well.' Poppy defended her friend. Seeing two people together in a canteen was jumping to conclusions, and Kate had acted on a little more than that.

'Uh... I didn't notice that.' Dylan walked across the room, sitting down opposite her. 'Here's the full story. Jeannie and I *were* seeing each other a couple of years ago. She's moved on now, but we're still friends. Her sister has epilepsy and she has frequent fits. She's just found out that she's a candidate for fibre optic laser therapy.'

Poppy swallowed down the unwelcome wave of relief that washed over her. 'I've heard a lot about that.'

'I saw it done up in Edinburgh, at the Great Northern Hospital. Far less invasive than conventional surgery and patients have a much faster and better recovery. But neither Jeannie or her sister know much about it, and they don't really understand her surgeon's recommendations. I told Jeannie I'd be happy to get the notes and test results and give a second opinion.'

Stupid. Poppy could feel herself reddening now. She'd not only been wrong, but she'd betrayed her own dismay at the thought of Dylan being involved with someone else.

'Sorry.' She ventured onto safer ground. 'Is Jeannie's sister all right?'

'Since Jeannie knows how everything works, she was able to push through the request for her sister's test results and I saw her on Thursday evening. I reviewed everything, and I agree entirely with her surgeon—he just hadn't explained the options all that well. When I talked it through with them, they both understood why he'd made his recommendations. Jeannie texted me this morning to say that her sister's feeling much better about everything and has decided to go ahead with the surgery.'

At least he didn't produce his phone and show her the text. That would be too humiliating for words.

'Got it. I'm the bad guy, Dylan. I can only apologise.'

He reached forward suddenly, the tips of his fingers almost touching hers. Not quite, but the effect was still electric. 'No, you're not the bad guy. I should have explained when I said I couldn't make lunch on Tuesday, but it was the only time that Jeannie and I were both free and she and her sister were both stressing out about things.'

'You don't need to tell me anything, Dylan. This is Jeannie's business, and her sister's. Not mine.' The words tasted bitter because Dylan had done exactly the right thing, and she'd jumped to the wrong conclusion so easily.

'You need to be able to trust me. I hadn't realised that Kate had seen me give Jeannie a hug, and I guess that if two people have already been in a relationship then there's a slightly different level of reserve. I wish Kate had asked me, but she's your friend. That means taking your side and talking to you first.'

'I may just kill her the next time I see her...' Poppy joked, shrugging awkwardly. If he wasn't careful, Dylan was going to end up far too good to be true.

'Don't. Please.' His blue eyes were suddenly clear and thoughtful. How could she have doubted him? 'Whatever Kate thinks about me, she's probably right.'

'You care about what anyone thinks, all of a sudden?' Another question that seemed to have slipped past the usual filters. Poppy couldn't help liking the way they always made Dylan smile.

'I care about what you think. And that *you* care about what I do.'

Poppy stared at him wordlessly. She couldn't think of a reply which didn't betray everything she'd been thinking and feeling. Dylan seemed to see her confusion, and thankfully didn't push for an answer.

'It's only till your lift gets mended, Poppy. Let's take it one day at a time, eh? Perhaps I could interest you in another cup of tea, in a brazen attempt to get you to stick around for a bit longer...?'

Poppy had been jealous. Dylan had seen it in her face, and he'd had to stop himself from smiling at the thought.

It was a new perspective. He'd always felt that jealousy was one step away from possessiveness, and two from commitment, and as such he reckoned it was a major red flag. But he'd welcomed Poppy's jealousy. In his head he regretted the hurt it had caused her, but his heart took an irrational pleasure in it.

And...instead of wordlessly skirting around the issue, making up their minds that this was one area of incompatibility that would push them further apart, it had brought them a step closer. This relationship was demanding more from him than he'd ever offered to anyone, and it came as a surprise that suddenly he knew how to give it.

It came as a surprise that he *wanted* to give it as well. Dylan was beginning to wonder whether Poppy might be the woman who peeled the spots from this leopard's back and applied a few new ones.

His hand shook as he made the tea, even the familiar process of boiling a kettle seeming somehow new and different. They sat together in the kitchen, making a list of all the things she needed from her flat, and then Dylan encouraged Poppy to add a few things to make her feel more at home here.

He stopped off to do a weekly shop on the way back and when he returned to the flat he heard Poppy's voice in the kitchen. His hands full, he kicked the door closed behind him and found her staring at her phone.

'You know that Oliver Shaw's daughter Kayley was in a car accident during the week?' Poppy looked up at him, and Dylan left the carrier bags where he'd dumped them on the counter.

'Yeah, I went down to Intensive Care to see them when I heard.' Dylan had worked with both Oliver and his ex-wife Lauren, who both specialised in reconstructive surgery. 'This must be tearing them to pieces, Kayley's twelve weeks pregnant.'

Poppy nodded. 'Yes, Lauren told me. I left a message for her, saying there was no need to call back, but so she'd know I was thinking of them. But she's just called me.' She looked up at Dylan. 'And all I could think of to say to you was to ask about your current sleeping arrangements.'

'That's different. We're all thinking of Oliver and Lauren, even if we don't talk about it. Is there any news?'

'Kayley's stable but she's still in a coma. The baby…only time will tell but right now Kayley's still pregnant. I said that I was staying with you for a while, and that we were both thinking of them. I knew you'd want me to send your best wishes as well.'

Dylan nodded. 'Thanks. I was going to suggest we called together, later on, just to keep their phone time down a bit. But it's better that Lauren called when she wanted to talk.'

Poppy got to her feet, walking towards him. 'It's made me realise what's really important, Dylan.' She caught his hand between hers, laying it carefully on one side of her stomach. Dylan felt their daughter kicking almost immediately and everything else in the world melted away.

'She's lively this morning.'

'I think she's saying hello to her dad.' Poppy

laid her head on his shoulder and the feeling took his breath away. The scent of her hair, feeling their baby kick. He put his arm around her shoulders and she snuggled against him.

This. Just this. There was nothing more that he wanted. And then Poppy grinned up at him, and he realised that her smile had been missing from his list of life's necessities.

'Just be there for her when she needs you, Dylan. I'm tendering my resignation as your intimacy co-ordinator.'

Poppy was joking about it, and that was a very good sign.

'What if I'm not planning on any intimacies for the foreseeable future?' That wasn't quite true. The one person he wanted to be intimate with, in so many different ways, was Poppy. But she'd already pointed out to him that wasn't on her agenda, and it would be wrong of him to mention it.

'I hear that board games are a good distraction.'

Dylan chuckled, feeling the baby move beneath his fingers. Maybe their baby girl was giving this new understanding her seal of approval. 'I have board games. You want some distraction?'

He saw Poppy's usual response to a challenge

firing up in her eyes. 'I have to warn you about my competitive streak.'

'You have a competitive streak?' Humour twinkled in his eyes. 'That's good, because you're just about to face your nemesis…'

CHAPTER ELEVEN

THE LAST FEW days had been exactly what Poppy needed. When Dylan had gone into work the following week it provided a framework for her. She could rest as much as she wanted during the day, and Dylan was there to share the evenings with her. Preparing dinner and eating then staying awake to talk might be simple pleasures, but they were spiced with a heady attraction that made time spent with Dylan something to look forward to.

It had been a mixed blessing, though. She'd lain awake at night, thinking that this was so like the life she'd had with Nate. The one she'd promised she wouldn't have with anyone else.

Promised Nate? Or promised herself? Maybe it was a little of both. All of the promises in the world hadn't allowed Nate to stay, and as her relationship with Dylan had become more precious to her Poppy had begun to realise how much she feared losing him.

But getting up in the morning, seeing Dylan's

smile as he rushed out of the door to work, made her brave. Cooking for him, enjoying his appreciation of their evening meal, turned her into a warrior queen who could face any kind of peril. And then the nights alone, broken by discomfort and regular visits to the bathroom, let in all of her fears again.

'Craniotomy.' On the day before Christmas Eve that wasn't a commonly heard greeting, but it made Poppy sit up straight. Dylan had been sharing his days at work with her, taking her through some of the complex procedures he'd performed. It wasn't quite as compelling as doing them herself, but it was good to talk about something that took her mind off her ever-changing body and made her feel like someone with a brain.

'Really? It was an emergency?'

Dylan nodded, slinging his overcoat across the back of the sofa, leaning down to deposit his briefcase on the cushion next to Poppy's feet. 'Yes. Very successful. You want to hear about it?'

She nodded. 'Yes, please. I have a large pot of goulash in the oven, and it'll be another forty-five minutes until it's ready.'

'Okay. I'm just going to make some tea and I'll be right with you.'

He walked over to the kitchen, reappearing carrying two cups of tea. He'd taken off his

jacket and rolled up the sleeves of his white shirt,
and when he sat down on the other end of the
long sofa he slipped off his shoes. One of his
plain navy-blue socks had a green toe and heel,
and the toe and heel of the other was red. Poppy
couldn't help smiling.

'You've got another pair just like that?'

Dylan grinned. 'Yep. Green and red are good
Christmas colours, aren't they?'

'Make sure you don't get the two pairs mixed
up. I never had you down as someone who wears
odd socks.'

'Seems you didn't have me down as a lot of
things.' He made that sound as if it wasn't quite
a rebuke, but he was right. Poppy had always
looked at his immaculate surface, never allowing herself to wonder what lay beneath it.

He reached for his briefcase, opening it and
drawing out the spiral-bound notepad that he
used to jot down the salient points of his day.
Poppy felt her toes begin to curl with anticipa-
tion. Dylan smelled so nice and he looked gorgeous too. Lean in all the right places, but his
shoulders and arms were bulked with muscle.
Her own body confidence felt a bit like a swinging barometer right now, some days partially
sunny and others freezing rain. But it was nice
to have him around and dream…

'Ow!' Pain suddenly shot through the arch of

one foot and along her calf. She could feel her toes continuing to curl into a solid, painful ball and when Poppy tried to reach them she couldn't. 'Ow! Cramp… My foot!'

Dylan's briefcase fell from his lap, scattering papers onto the floor. He took hold of her foot, stripping off her sock, and straightening her toes. That felt better and when he slipped his hand under her knee, expertly straightening her leg and pushing her foot upwards, the pain in her calf muscle suddenly abated.

'That's…good. Thank you.' Poppy went to pull away from him and felt another twinge running along the side of her foot.

'Don't move. If it feels better just stay there.'

Poppy decided to take his advice. 'I'm glad that one of us can reach my feet…' She gave in to the feeling of his fingers probing her leg. Not actually touching her skin, but even through the fabric of her leggings it felt almost like a caress.

'You've been getting cramps a lot?'

'A bit more than usual. No more than ex-pected—you don't need to go and fetch your doctor's hat.'

Something ignited in his eyes. A tenderness that seemed to come from the man and not the doctor. He increasingly had the ability to slip out from behind all of the labels she'd given him—

doctor, friend, uncle—and she was in the presence of a man. The father of her child.

One thumb was under her toes, stopping them from beginning to curl again. The other hand was on her calf muscle, probing gently.

'That's it. Right there.'

He nodded. 'I can feel it.' His touch became firmer, a little more searching. More pleasurable…

Poppy amended the thought quickly. More therapeutic. She could feel him working the muscle, which responded to his gentle fingers and began to relax.

'Your toes are cold.' He'd turned his attention to her foot now. When he let go of her toes they started to curl again, and he pulled them back straight. 'Hold on. I'll just get something to warm them up a bit.'

He laid her foot back down onto the sofa and got to his feet. Dylan spent only two minutes in the bathroom before he emerged with a bowl of steaming water, a flannel and a towel, but Poppy's muscles were already beginning to cramp again. He spread the towel over a cushion, propping her foot up, and then dipped the flannel into the water, wringing it out. Then he wrapped the warm fabric around her foot, massaging her toes.

Heaven. Pure heaven. There was none of the reassuring technology of the hospital but the traditional techniques had a thing or two going for them as well. Watching Dylan as he concentrated on the task in hand, the whisper of a smile on his lips as he felt her begin to respond and relax. Suddenly her feet were no longer a distant country, they were centres of warmth and feeling.

What couldn't they do with this moment? The thought of the forbidden was sending warm tingles down her spine.

'Your ankles aren't too swollen,' he murmured and Poppy nodded.

'It feels much better, thank you.'

He tapped her other foot lightly with his finger in an unspoken invitation. Poppy cordially ignored the fact that she felt no trace of cramp in it and shifted round, propping it onto the soft towel.

He knew. Poppy saw a sudden flash in his blue eyes and the trace of a smile. The way he stripped her other sock off seemed slightly more sensual, more sure of himself. She'd almost forgotten how it felt when her body responded to someone entirely of its own accord. When just a look or a smile was enough to start the slow, delicious journey into arousal.

Maybe he felt that too. He warmed and massaged her other foot with the same gentle fingers, but somehow it was less relaxing and more pleasurable. Then she felt his thumb pressing on the soft hollow beneath her ankle…

'Too much?' His fingers stilled suddenly.

It wasn't enough. Poppy pulled herself back from the warm tide of sensation that was making her toes tingle. Dylan's gaze found hers and she saw everything that was unspoken between them in his eyes.

'It's fine. It feels much better.'

She wanted so badly to reach for him. There was something about the way he was looking at her which made her feel beautiful. As if he wanted her touch just as much as she wanted his. That suddenly seemed so much more important than her doubts and fears.

Then his smiling look of regret brought Poppy back down to earth. This couldn't happen. They mustn't even say it, because that would acknowledge something that neither of them could handle. But Dylan handled *not* saying it really well.

'We'll leave it there then?'

Poppy gave him a smiling nod. He dried her toes with the towel, then put her socks back on and covered her legs with a throw from the back of one of the armchairs.

'Thanks, Dylan. I don't think I ever fully appreciated the value of foot care before I was pregnant.'

'And that's just the time you can't reach them.' He chuckled. 'One of the more annoying tricks that life plays on a person. Did you call to find out whether your lift has stopped playing annoying tricks?'

'Yes, I did. It's been mended and working fine now. Hence my special goulash, as a thank you.' Hence maybe allowing herself to forget that she and Dylan were bound by the baby inside her, but still very different people.

'We'll need to get up early so you'll be home in time for your father to pick you up for Christmas.'

Poppy shook her head. 'Actually, there's been a slight change of plan. I video-conferenced with them today, and they're snowed in. It happens— the smaller villages near to Cologne get quite a bit of snow in the winter.'

'So they won't be back? Come over to Sam and Sophie's with me on Christmas Day.'

'Thanks, but...' That might be a step too far, and she'd been taking too many of those lately. 'They're trying again tomorrow. Mum says the roads should be clearer then, and they should make it home by the evening. Dad'll come and pick me up on Christmas morning.'

Dylan nodded. 'Okay. But give me a ring if they don't make it.'

Poppy nodded, leaning forward to catch his

hand. A brief squeeze and then he was on his feet, picking up the bowl and flannel to take back to the bathroom.

Dylan was going to miss Poppy. Those early nights when he went up to the gallery and lay on his bed, reading or watching TV with the sound turned down and subtitles switched on. Listening for her. Keeping watch over her and the baby as if he were a real dad and not just a biological father.

He was already head-over-heels in love with the baby girl that Poppy was carrying, and things were moving fast in that direction with Poppy as well. He'd shared his flat before, partners had come and then gone again, but they'd always left the place much as they'd found it. Poppy had made it into a home, turned his kitchen into a comforting refuge, filled with warmth and the scent of cooking and the Christmas tree into a twinkling source of light that seemed to radiate all of the magic of the season.

There was a price to be paid for that, though. Those delicious moments when they stepped over the line they'd drawn for themselves had given him a glimpse of what he and Poppy could be together. But however right that had felt, it had also felt right to draw back again. If he couldn't protect her from the possibility that he might fail her, then how could he expect to protect her from the thousand other things that could hurt Poppy or their child?

Time was ticking slowly forward. Through the night and into the dawn, when Dylan rose from his bed and took a shower. Steadily marking a beat as they ate breakfast, and checked that Poppy had packed everything. When she put on her red coat, adding a red hat with a white pompom, and picked up the fairy from her post by the bed in the spare room his flat seemed to darken.

Snow tumbled against the windscreen as they drove, and Poppy's phone rang in her pocket. 'Unknown number. I bet it's a scammer or a sales call.'

'On Christmas Eve? When it's snowing? Far more likely to be a lost reindeer wanting directions.' Dylan grinned and she laughed, answering the call.

Someone spoke at the other end of the line, and suddenly she was all smiles. 'Thank you so much. Give Lauren and Oliver my love, won't you. And from Dylan Harper too… No, it's okay, you can tick him off your list. I'll let him know right now.'

'Whose list have you just ticked me off? And is that what I think it is?'

'Yes! That was a friend of Lauren's calling round to let us all know that Kayley's woken up.

She's weak, of course, and she'll need care but she's going to be all right. The baby's fine too.'

'Wonderful news.' Suddenly it really *was* Christmas, and there was hope in the air.

'I sent my love, and yours too. We'll be able to pop in and see Kayley when she gets out of the ICU.'

'Who said that there's no Christmas magic, eh?'

'Dylan! I distinctly remember hearing you tell a student that there was no magic in medicine. Just hard work and precision.'

He laughed. 'It's never too late to learn…'

Poppy was bubbling with excitement by the time they reached her front door. Dylan had made sure that her plants and the Christmas tree were watered and left everything tidy when he'd come to pick up her things. He'd brought a bag of food from his own fridge and as soon as the place warmed up a bit everything would be back the way it should be. Apart from just one thing…

'You want me to put the fairy back onto the tree?' Poppy was still holding the fairy between her gloved hands.

'Yes. Thank you so much, Dylan.'

He could just reach… Dylan stretched up and fixed the fairy back at the top of the tree. Poppy was clapping and laughing the same way that she had last time, her face glowing with joy. Everything was the same, and he wasn't really losing her after all. He turned, putting his arm loosely around her shoulders, and Poppy looked up at him, her eyes moist with tears.

Good tears. The tears which overflowed from a heart that was full of joy. One of them escaped her eye and Dylan wiped it away with his finger. Tenderness overwhelmed him, and he brushed his lips against her cheek.

She was still looking up into his gaze, melting him from the inside out. Passion began to stir, something new and all-encompassing that made everything else seem like a mere murmur of feeling. He felt her fingers pressing softly on the back of his neck and couldn't resist. Gently, he gathered her in his arms, leaning down, and Poppy kissed his mouth.

A real kiss, not the kind that was gone before it had ever really been there. Sweet, a little hesitant, but full of Poppy's firm resolve. He kissed her again, and this time Poppy responded with all the hunger that he felt. Slowly they deepened the kiss, in a complex dance of questions and answers that felt natural and right.

'You're so beautiful.' He brushed a strand of hair from her cheek, kissing the skin beneath it. Dylan knew she needed to hear that. He'd seen the way she turned the corners of her mouth down when she awkwardly sat down, reaching helplessly for her swollen ankles. Poppy loved being pregnant, and it was everything she wanted, but sometimes his compliments fell on deaf ears.

But this time she believed him. She was looking up at him with that clear warmth in her eyes which held nothing back. She must feel his desire. He couldn't have feigned the way his body was reacting to hers if he'd tried.

'She feels us…' Dylan had been dimly aware that the baby was moving but when Poppy twined her fingers in his, placing his hand on the side of her stomach, it felt as if the little girl had decided it was time for a workout.

He kissed her cheek, feeling almost embarrassed, and Poppy laughed at his sudden hesitancy. 'She feels the warmth, Dylan. She doesn't know what's on your mind.'

Poppy knew, though. And when she kissed him again it was quite clear that she had the exact same thought as he did. Her body was a little busy at the moment, making a miracle, but the look in her eyes told him that one day, maybe soon, she'd have time just for him.

And their daughter was a part of that. Cocooned safely between them, maybe feeling the heat that had been absent when she'd been conceived. Now that Dylan was getting used to the idea, his thoughts were running away with him, leapfrogging over the years to find that Poppy was there with him, a constant and loving presence. Someone who could give him everything that his heart and his body craved.

It was too soon for an *I love you*. That would surely come later. But when Dylan kissed her he felt love in his heart, and saw it in Poppy's gaze. He fell to his knees, resting his cheek against her swollen stomach. If Poppy's love was more than he'd ever need in his life, this was something different but more. A next step, taken before their first, which made everything suddenly come together.

Dylan rose, seeking the warmth in her eyes, the tender feel of her lips again. But Poppy had looked up and seen something beyond the cocoon that had formed around them.

He didn't need to turn—he could see it in her face. Poppy's wedding photograph stood in the alcove next to the fireplace behind him. A reminder of all the things that might tear them apart if they took the risk of loving each other. He tried to reach for her, forget the feelings that engendered, but he couldn't.

Dylan's kiss had been everything. Everything that Poppy had thought she'd never feel again...

No. It had been more than that. For those sweet moments it had been Dylan alone. Just him, like a first love that hadn't yet learned how to fear loss. It had seemed impossible that she might start something new when she was so heavily pregnant, but he'd made it seem so right. As if suddenly all the pieces in her life had clicked together.

And then there was the desire. The feeling that he found her immeasurably beautiful. Her aching legs and complaining back were suddenly lost in the wash of wanting him. Wanting to explore that hard, perfect body of his, and knowing what her touch might do.

But she'd looked up. Hesitated and then baulked. Maybe if he'd turned her head away, gone back to the beginning again and talked her through it, the way he'd done with some of the other issues they'd faced, it would have been different. But Dylan simply didn't do that with his relationships, and there was no way that Poppy could do it on her own.

'That was nice...' His smile had lost its ardour, and seemed like part of a plan for what he needed to do next. And *nice* really didn't cover it. It was practically an insult to what had gone between them.

But Poppy couldn't go back now. Guilt was sweeping over her like a great wave, and Dylan had been thrown clear and was too far away now for her to reach. She'd lost Nate, the man she'd promised to always love. And if she could lose Nate then she could lose Dylan as well.

'Yes.' She stepped away from him, looking helplessly around the room for something that urgently needed to be done. When the earth had moved between them, surely it had left some trace... But there was nothing. Even the fairy on the tree looked serene and unruffled.

'You must have things to do. I should let you get on.'

Dylan didn't look convinced. 'I don't have much to do. Some present wrapping...'

Present wrapping on Christmas Eve sounded nice, but right now even the thought of that festive warmth was an impossible agony. 'I'll be okay. Go and wrap your presents.'

He nodded, picking up his jacket and walking into the hallway. Poppy stopped in the doorway that led into the sitting room. No fond goodbyes at the front door.

'Happy Christmas,' she remembered to call after him and he turned. She could see the quickly hidden scepticism at the idea in his face.

'You too. Call me if there's anything you need. I'll see you after Christmas.'

They both knew that neither of them would call over Christmas. And right now *after Christmas* seemed far too far away to even think about.

But Poppy nodded and Dylan opened the front door, letting himself out.

Maybe she should have run to him. Poppy adjusted the thought to her current best effort of a brisk walk. Dylan was obviously hurt, and she should have explained. Given him one loving touch to reassure him. But she couldn't. Any relationship she had with Dylan would be based on the pretence that she was able to love again without dreading its consequences, and that wasn't something that Poppy wanted for either of them.

She walked back into the sitting room, picking up her wedding photograph. Nate's face was shining, so proud and happy. And she'd been so in love with him. He was gone now, but that moment would last for ever...

Suddenly she felt it. A wave that started at the top of her uterus and moved downwards. Poppy put her hand on her stomach, feeling it harden as the pain increased. Any second now...

It didn't stop. She let out a whimper, trying to breathe, and the picture frame fell from her hand, clattering against the plant pot and then slipping down behind the sideboard. Somewhere in the distance she heard breaking glass, but instinct had taken over and all she could feel was the pain.

'Not yet, sweetheart...' She gasped out the words, knowing that they'd make no difference.

This baby was coming, and Dylan wasn't here. Poppy looked for her phone, remembering that it was still packed in her handbag in the hallway.

Then she saw the remote for the door, right in front of her, where she'd left it six days ago on the sideboard. She picked it up, thumbing the intercom. Dylan would be going through the main doors on his way out, and surely he'd hear the buzz.

Unless he'd already gone. The pain had subsided now, and Poppy gingerly took two steps towards the window. His car was still parked outside in the street. She thumbed the intercom again.

'Dylan! Dylan, I need you…' She kept her thumb on the buzzer, gasping as the second contraction began to build. This one was stronger, and she yelped, holding onto the intercom for dear life.

Breathe. Just breathe. She could get to her phone and call the midwife. Poppy got as far as the sofa and decided to rest for a moment, bending forward and planting her hands on the armrest. That felt a little better…

Then she heard Dylan's voice, followed by a loud rapping on the front door. 'Poppy…? Poppy, press the door release. Let me in…'

She fumbled for the intercom, almost dropping it, before she managed to disengage the lock on the front door. She heard it slam behind him and his hurried footsteps in the hall, and then he was there, gently supporting her.

'Just breathe—everything's okay.'

'No, it's not!' Poppy immediately regretted snapping at him. 'I feel a bit better, though. Maybe if I sit down for a few minutes.'

He took her arm and she leaned on him gratefully as he walked her a couple more steps and helped her sit down. Poppy flopped to one side, stretching out, and he lifted her feet up onto the cushions.

'I'll take you to the hospital.' He was smiling now. Reassuring.

'Maybe it's…' Maybe it wasn't a false alarm. Poppy wasn't sure. 'The leaflet says to call first.'

'I don't care what the leaflet says. I'm a doctor.'

He must have seen her grimace, and laid his hand lightly on her stomach as the pain began to build again. Dylan gripped her hand, and she hung on to him.

'You're a neurologist.' Finally, it subsided and she could trust herself to speak without screaming the words at him.

'Yeah, and I did my rotations at medical school, the same as you did. *And* I've been brushing up over the last few weeks.'

He had? 'You didn't tell *me*.'

'No, I didn't. Just breathe, will you. And when you get the next contraction I'll be needing you to make as much noise as you can. Let it all out.' He looked at his watch. Dylan was clearly taking note of how long it was between each contraction, and it must be less than five minutes...

She didn't need to ask. He had that all under control, and her body was beckoning her towards a greater, more all-encompassing task.

'Whatever you think, Mr Harper.'

Did he just roll his eyes? She'd have a word with him about his bedside manner when this was all over.

'Thank you, Ms Evans. You concentrate on what you're doing, and leave the rest to me.'

CHAPTER TWELVE

'*THE REST*' WAS accomplished with startling ease. Before Poppy knew it, she was downstairs and in the car. Dylan took the backstreet route to avoid the Christmas Eve traffic, and fifteen minutes later they were parked outside the maternity unit at the hospital.

'My notes...' Poppy suddenly remembered that she'd been supposed to bring them with her.

'I've got them.'

'My phone...' At some point she was going to have to call her parents to let them know where she was.

'That's in your handbag. Which you're holding. Breathe...' He'd seen her grimace and he got into the back seat of the car with her, waiting for the contraction to subside. Then he hurried to the entrance of the unit, returning almost immediately with a wheelchair.

Everything was happening much faster than she'd expected. The onset of contractions and the way the midwife took them straight through

to one of the birth suites, as Dylan quickly updated her on the interval between contractions.

'Your birth partner, Poppy. Can we make a
call for you?'

Poppy was still struggling to keep up. 'My
sister... But she's on her way back from Germany.' This baby wasn't going to wait for that.
She turned to Dylan.

'Dylan. Please...' Maybe this was too much
to ask of him, but he smiled, taking her hand.

'With you all the way.'

Dylan had been many things today. A spurned
lover. A doctor. A birth partner. And now...
Now he was a bemused and besotted father. His
daughter had been in a hurry to make her way
into the world, and little more than three hours
after he'd heard Poppy's voice on the intercom,
and run up six flights of stairs, the baby girl
was born.

There was quiet activity around them, but for
once he didn't care. He was dimly aware that all
the correct medical procedures were being followed, and he wasn't a part of that. He and Poppy
were in their own small bubble, both focused on
the tiny baby that lay on her chest.

'You did so well. Both of you,' he murmured.
Dylan couldn't imagine ever tearing himself
away from this moment. It would follow him

always, somewhere to go whenever the going got tough. And he imagined that it would, although even that had lost its sting right now.

'Do you want to hold her?' Poppy's gaze met his suddenly.

More than anything. He didn't want to break the skin-against-skin connection between Poppy and the baby, which was keeping the little one warm and contented under the thin blanket that covered them both. Nor did he want to ask for more than Poppy wanted to give—he'd only even been here by chance. But acting considerately and well was being drowned out by an instinct to hold his daughter in his arms that just wouldn't let go of him.

'Do you know her name yet?' Dylan avoided the question.

'Listen. What do you hear?'

Quiet voices around them. The subdued noise of the machine which was still monitoring Poppy's vital signs. He shot her a puzzled look, not wanting to direct her thoughts in any particular way other than where they wanted to go.

She smiled. 'What do you think of Belle?'

Now he heard it. The faint peal of Christmas bells, coming from one of the city churches that surrounded them. Ringing out hope for the future.

'I think it's perfect. It really suits her.'

Poppy chuckled. 'Along with Impatience. She really didn't want to wait any longer, did she. We can't really call her that, can we.'

Dylan shook his head. 'Not unless you like unusual middle names. Even then, it carries a few expectations.'

'She's perfect as she is. I have no expectations other than that she be loved for whoever she wants to be.'

She'd be loved. If Poppy wasn't planning on taking up residence in his heart, then it would be all for Belle. Dylan nodded his agreement, a conflict of emotions raging in his chest.

And then, suddenly, they fell quiet. Poppy had murmured a few words to the midwife, and she helped her to lift Belle and wrap her in a soft baby blanket. Then his daughter was placed carefully into his arms. Belle scrunched up her face and he felt her shifting against him, then she settled again as he stroked her head with his trembling fingers.

Cold air and the scrunch of a layer of snow beneath his feet wasn't quite enough to bring Dylan to his senses. But he could drive back to Poppy's flat, sorting out the things she'd need and packing them to take to her in hospital. Glancing across towards the photograph that had changed everything yesterday, he saw only a cracked plant pot and scattered broken leaves. When he went to investigate further, a trail of glass fragments led him to the broken picture frame, which had slid down behind the sideboard.

There were a few hours to kill before he was expected back. Poppy needed to rest and she'd wanted to call her family, to see what was happening with them and introduce them to Belle. Dylan moved the sideboard, clearing up the mess of broken glass and taking the plant to the kitchen to trim its bent stalks. He wound a few rounds of tape around the pot, the emergency surgery would have to do for the time being, and returned it to its place on the sideboard. Maybe a little water would help with the plant's recovery…

Anything. Think about anything, so you don't have to face the one thing that has to be faced. But the shattered frame was still waiting for him. When he picked it up he found that the mounting board had saved the photograph from any harm, and he could carefully extract it from the wreckage.

Poppy looked joyful. Her husband—Dylan still couldn't bear to think of him by name—had all the signs of a happiness that Dylan had presumed to feel. If it had been anyone else then he could have fought for Poppy, but not this man.

Not the one who'd captured her whole heart, leaving Dylan out in the cold.

Dylan frowned. Now, he was just feeling sorry for himself, digging down to find all the feelings of rejection—that childish certainty that if he'd been better and more worthy of his father's love then he never would have left. He was the one who'd broken their agreement, not Poppy. She'd compromised with him when she hadn't needed to, let him share the first moments of Belle's life and promised that he would be able to share more. She could no more give him her heart than fly in the air, because it belonged to someone else.

Now he had something to do. If he couldn't be entirely happy then at least he could be busy, and that thought always made him feel strong again. He could live up to his promises, and that would make him the man his father never had been. Belle would have every last piece of him that he could give, and Poppy and Nate would have his respect.

Dylan had come back to the hospital with her things, and Poppy had made it clear that he was welcome to stay as long as he liked. He'd been kind and caring towards her, understanding that she was still floating on a sea of drugs and emotion. And he'd watched Belle hungrily, waiting for any chance he might have to hold her. Poppy had gently tried to wake her, and the little girl's eyes had remained firmly shut. Then somehow her dreams had wakened her, and Dylan had taken her, walking her up and down until she fell asleep again in his arms.

'She's had a big day.' Poppy couldn't get enough of seeing him with Belle at the moment. 'Did you see her eyes?'

'They may well change.' A note of uncertainty sounded in Dylan's voice. He was clearly hoping that Belle might have inherited something of his.

'I hope not. They're such a gorgeous blue.' Poppy had deliberately chosen a donor with the same eye and hair colouring as her, so that she wouldn't be wondering whether the baby was like her or its father. But now that Belle was here, had a name and a personality all of her own, none of that mattered. She could do a lot worse than inherit her father's blond hair and blue eyes.

Dylan bent to plant the tenderest of kisses on Belle's forehead. 'With any luck she'll have your determination to do things her own way. If she doesn't, you'll just have to teach her.'

'I'm planning on doing things one day at a time at the moment.' Right now, the next twenty years were going to have to take care of themselves. 'They may well be discharging us tomorrow, so Belle will be having her first Christmas at home.'

'I'll be here in the morning to collect you both. What time?' Dylan looked up at her.

'No! You've got someone else waiting for you on Christmas Day. Thomas is going to need his bricks, along with his uncle to help him put them together.'

'There's plenty of time to do both. Sam and Sophie usually spread the present opening out a bit and I can be there for the afternoon. Did you call your mum and dad?'

Poppy turned the corners of her mouth down. 'They started out this morning, but it began to snow really heavily and they had to turn back. Dad was ready to set off again when he heard Belle had been born but I insisted they wait until after Christmas. I don't want them taking any risks.'

Dylan nodded. 'Sensible. In that case I'll definitely be here tomorrow. I put the carrycot into my car, just in case you were going to need it.'

'And…' Poppy frowned at him. The carrycot hadn't been among the things he'd brought up to the unit. 'You're not going to make me stay here until you arrive by holding my carrycot ransom, are you?'

He grinned. 'Well, you're definitely not going to need it tonight. And I'll be here first thing in the morning…'

True to his word, Dylan was at the hospital early on Christmas Day. There were a few unfamiliar faces among the staff on duty, and they were clearly busy, but everything went like clockwork. She'd be going home for Christmas.

That wouldn't be quite as joyful an occasion as it sounded. But at least Belle would be introduced to the smiling porcelain figure on top of the tree, and maybe she would sprinkle a little fairy dust their way. She dressed Belle in one of the sleepsuits that Dylan had brought from Poppy's ever-growing collection, adding the festive red and white hat that the hospital had given her, over her soft fuzz of pale blonde hair.

They were ready. There were smiling goodbyes and 'Happy Christmas's.

'You could drive just a little faster, Dylan.' He'd made sure that everything was done in Poppy's own time, even though he must be keen to get to his brother's house.

'Nah…' He turned into Regent Street and suddenly there was another first for Belle. The usually busy road was almost empty but for a few cars, and the Christmas lights twinkled above their heads. Angels appeared to be hovering over them. And… Christmas bells at the top of each lamppost. In the unexpected quiet, Poppy could almost hear them chime.

Even if she'd been awake, Belle wouldn't have been able to see them yet. But Poppy could and she'd remember this piece of Christmas magic. Dylan drove the whole length of the street and then turned back, heading for Poppy's flat.

As they rode up to the sixth floor, Poppy felt a quiver of excitement grow. Dylan stopped at the front door, carefully taking Belle from the baby carrier and putting her into Poppy's arms. Then he opened the door, standing back so that she could carry her daughter into her new home.

Dylan must have been here already this morning, and the place was warm, the lights of the Christmas tree twinkling out into an overcast and gloomy day. He left Belle and Poppy alone in the sitting room and Poppy leaned back in her seat, glad that her body felt a little lighter now, and testing out the new aches and pains from the birth. Home. She was home, and all the hope and joy of a new little life was stirring beside her now.

Dylan was warming some mince pies and brought them through with two cups of tea, gulping his down as quickly as he could. Poppy knew what that was all about and beckoned him over, putting Belle into his arms. She couldn't get enough of the goofy smile that spread over his face when he held her.

'I bought a turkey crown and that won't need too long in the oven. There are vegetables and all the trimmings in the fridge…' He seemed determined to make today as festive as possible. 'I can put it all into the freezer if you don't feel like it.'

'I have all I need for Christmas, Dylan.' Suddenly she wasn't sure *what* she needed. After all of the emotion of the last few days, the vulnerability and the memory of his kiss…

Some time alone. Time to let her crowded head make sense of it all and settle into the life she'd planned for her and Belle. And she couldn't keep Dylan from his family at Christmastime. That was the life *he* wanted, the one that she'd selfishly snatched him away from over the last few weeks.

'You should go. You can make Christmas lunch with your family if you go now.'

Dylan shook his head. 'And leave you on your own?'

'I'm not on my own, Dylan. Belle and I are just starting to get to know each other. Your nephew's going to be so disappointed if he doesn't see you, and there's that special present for your mum that you were telling me about. She's going to want to hug both of her sons when she sees her new car...'

Why did that make her feel so empty? Christmas spent together had never been a part of the plan and right now, when they were still feeling their way, wasn't the time to start playing things by ear.

'But...what if something happens? I should be here, with you.'

Should. If Dylan had said that he *wanted* to be here then maybe—only maybe—Poppy would have changed her mind.

'Nothing's going to happen. I have a number to call if I have any worries, and I promise I'll let you know too. I want you to go, Dylan.'

Maybe she could have said that a little more tactfully, because Poppy could see the hurt in his face. But suddenly she really *did* want him to go. They both had their own lives, and becoming dependent on each other really wasn't the right thing for Dylan, or for her.

He didn't argue. Dylan had never expected anything, it had always been Poppy who had offered. He got to his feet, kissing Belle's forehead and putting her back into the baby carrier.

'That's the deal, isn't it?' His face was impassive, suddenly. Unreadable.

'Yes, Dylan. That's what we decided was best for both of us. Give me a call after Christmas and let me know when you'd like to come and see Belle. Maybe we'll take her out for her first walk to the park, eh?'

He nodded, picking up his jacket and feeling in the pocket for her spare keys, which he laid on the coffee table. 'Goodbye, Poppy.'

Dylan hadn't said another word as she'd walked through the hallway with him, letting him out of the flat. Poppy had returned to the sitting room, which suddenly seemed a lot darker and dimmer, and reminded herself that she'd never reckoned on this being easy. But she'd done the right thing. When he arrived at his brother's and found that the people he loved had been waiting for him he'd see that.

But there was something about the finality of his words that had cut like a knife. She leaned over, and Belle's eyes fluttered open for a moment. 'Don't you worry, sweetheart. He said goodbye to me. He's never going to say that to you. Do you want to come and see our Christmas tree?'

Belle's eyes closed again. That would be a no, then. The fairy was going to have to wait before she was introduced to the newest member of the family. Poppy stared at the tree, trying to muster up a little Christmas spirit. The presents beneath it were still waiting for her family's return…

And there was another one, added to the pile. Poppy wondered whether that had been one that she'd forgotten having wrapped, and then decided not, since the blue and gold paper was unfamiliar. She walked over to the tree, bending slowly to pick it up, and looked at the tag.

Just one word.

Poppy

And it was in Dylan's handwriting. What had he gone and done?

The shape, the feel of it were familiar. Poppy returned to the sofa, hardly daring to open it. Not daring to look at the empty space on the dresser. A stab of guilt dug at her heart when she realised that she'd forgotten all about that.

She carefully loosened the sticky tape on the present. Stalling for time, hoping this wasn't what she thought it was. Ripping the paper, as she usually did, seemed wrong but she couldn't put the moment off for ever and the paper drifted in one piece to the floor, revealing her wedding photograph. As good as new, in a gorgeous silver frame.

Nate's gaze seemed to bore into her. Her mouthed apology didn't do any good, and she still felt terrible for forgetting him, excluding him from the moment when she brought the baby that they should have had together back home.

This was Dylan's final word. He knew that she

belonged with Nate and he'd accepted that. That hurt too, a lot more than it should.

'Belle...' Poppy laid the frame carefully down on the coffee table and turned to her daughter. The one person she'd never exclude from any part of her life. The little girl seemed to sense her mother's presence and maybe her mood too, and started to cry. Poppy picked her up, holding her against her chest and rocking her gently.

'No need for that, sweetheart. Everything's okay, I promise.' Tears were running down Poppy's cheeks too, but the instinct to comfort Belle was more powerful than anything else. 'Hush now, Belle. I love you...'

CHAPTER THIRTEEN

THAT WAS THAT, THEN. Dylan had dared to love Poppy, but he should have known that nothing ever came of a broken agreement. He had to move on. Or rather, move back. Somehow, he found it in himself to arrive at Sam's house with a smile on his face. Hug his mother and then catch Thomas up in his arms, swinging him round before he held him tightly to his chest.

But even his beloved nephew couldn't fill the empty space that Poppy had left. She and Belle had turned him into an adventurer, showing him that he could feel more than he'd ever thought he would. Now that he was back in a familiar place he couldn't settle.

'We've got some news.' Sam had poured them both a splash of brandy and taken Dylan out into the garage to inspect his latest project, a tree-house for Thomas that would be assembled in the spring.

'Yeah?' From the look on Sam's face it was

good news, and Dylan could certainly do with a little of that at the moment.

'Sophie's pregnant.'

'Yeah? That *is* good news.' Dylan clapped his brother on the back, hugging him. 'I didn't realise you were going back to the fertility clinic so soon.'

'You think we'd have done that without making you a part of it, like last time? After all this time spent trying, we finally managed to do it all on our own. Who'd have thought it?'

Dylan chuckled. 'You and Sophie always were the first team. I was just the second reserve.'

'Hey. You *know* you were always the first reserve, Dylan. We were going to tell you and Mum together, but I told Sophie that I wanted to tell you first. You'll have to act a bit surprised when we do tell her.'

Dylan chuckled, throwing his arms around his brother in another hug. 'Tell her soon, eh? I can't keep this to myself for too long. Now's good, isn't it…?'

'Not yet.'

Something prickled at the back of Dylan's neck. 'Why—is anything wrong?'

'No, everyone's fine. It's you I'm worried about. What's eating at you?'

'It's nothing. Hospital stuff…' Dylan's excuse for being late today had been to refer vaguely to having been at the hospital. No one had questioned that—they were used to him being called in from time to time.

'Must have been bad. You don't usually bring that home with you.'

Dylan shrugged. 'You know...'

'Funnily enough, I do. You can convince everyone else that you've just had a bad day at work, but I'm your brother. Twins' intuition.'

'Ah. So we really can read each other's minds, can we?'

When Dylan and Sam were teenagers they'd devised a code that allowed them to fool their friends. Maybe some of the appeal had been that reading each other's minds might make them inseparable. Two lost boys who would always have each other.

'Nah. I can read the look on your face when you think no one's looking your way.'

'Covert surveillance, then.'

It was no use. Sam wasn't going to give up, and Dylan didn't want him to. Sooner or later, he'd know about Poppy and Belle and he and Poppy had agreed weeks ago that it was okay to tell close friends and family. Sam fell into both those categories.

As soon as he started it all began to spill out, like a gush of frustrated emotion. The mix-up at the fertility clinic. How he and Poppy had carefully worked their way towards finding out what they wanted. Their agreement.

'And now you have feelings for her?' Sam was leaning back against the workbench, listening carefully.

Dylan drained the last drop of brandy from his glass, wishing for a moment that they'd brought the bottle out with them. 'I think so...'

'I'll take that as a *yes*. If you didn't then you'd know.'

That made sense.

'I love her, Sam. It's not just Belle, although she's...' Dylan shrugged. 'You know.'

'Yeah, I do. I love Sophie, and I love Thomas. It's not a popularity contest.'

Dylan nodded. 'So what's the answer, then?'

'Search me. If someone doesn't love you, then they don't love you. You can't cure that, Doc. You just have to accept it and do the best you can for everyone else concerned.'

'You always did handle Dad leaving better than I did...' Dylan turned the corners of his mouth down.

'Yeah? Tell that to Sophie—it would give her a laugh. We've had our moments, as you know, and it was generally over my habit of just letting things happen. You raged over it, Dylan, and that might well have been a more healthy reaction.'

Dylan chuckled. 'Just as well there were two

of us, then. Mum could take her pick over which one she felt like agreeing with at the time.'

Every instinct told him to fight right now, but if it couldn't work between him and Poppy then fighting would only make things worse. He had to get this right, there was no more room for mistakes.

'Sophie would say that *you* can take your pick. Sometimes you do have to accept things, but sometimes it's okay to fight—she's told me that enough times. Not that I'm admitting she's right or anything...' Sam grinned.

'No. Of course not.' Sophie had always been good for Sam, and the two of them had found their way together through everything that life had thrown at them. It occurred to Dylan that maybe acceptance would be a more loving thing to do in this situation. Give Poppy some space to work out what she really wanted. It was a new form of challenge that Dylan was unfamiliar with.

'Do you know what you're going to do next?' Sam asked.

'Not really. It's all too new to be able to put it together right now. But it was good to talk.'

'Well, I'm not wishing to break the moment... But you do know that if Thomas thinks we're idling around he'll be out here with a job for you to do. He's got a few construction projects of his own, now that he's opened all of his Christmas presents.'

Dylan nodded. He needed some time to think and the illusion of a happy Christmas had been difficult to maintain this year. But he'd do it, because there was really nothing else that he *could* do.

'Although Mum's dying to help him with the kit she got him.' Sam was watching him steadily. 'Did you see her face when he opened it?'

'Yeah.' Dylan summoned up a smile. 'She'll have another grandchild soon as well. She can do all the Christmassy things with them that she never got to do with us.'

'She's got another grandchild already, Dylan. We might not get to meet her, but Belle will always have a place with us if she wants it. And so will her mother. You know that, don't you.'

'Yeah, I know. I'm going to have to see how things pan out. Poppy did mention babysitting.'

'Okay, well, hold that thought, Dylan. Sophie and I aren't going to push our way in, but we're there for you and we're there for them as well. Always.'

The light in Sam's eyes was something new. Something different. His brother had learned to fight for their family, and maybe Dylan should follow his example and acknowledge that he had a choice about what to do next.

'Thanks. I don't know what else to say, but... thanks. Do we need to get back now?'

Sam shrugged. 'Like I said, Mum'll keep Thomas amused, and if he sees we're busy... Fancy helping me check the measurements for the treehouse?' He nodded towards the large oak tree in the back garden.

Maybe Sam really could read his mind. Climbing a tree with his brother sounded like a fine thing to do on Christmas Day.

Dylan grinned. 'Got an old jacket I can borrow...?'

'You are *so* busted, Poppy.'

Poppy let out a sigh. She'd cried for a while, and then slept for a while on the sofa. The phone had woken her, and Belle was shifting fitfully in her crib. Not quite awake enough to cry, but getting there.

'Kate...?'

'Yep. Valued friend and confidante, remember? Who didn't even get a picture of the baby... Your mum texted me. You sound sleepy—did I wake you?'

'Yes.' There was no point in being bad-tempered with Kate—she couldn't help it if she wasn't Dylan. 'I mean... That's okay, Belle's due a feed shortly. What did Mum say?'

'She said that she'd seen you and Belle via

video call, and wanted to know whether you were as well as you were making out. I texted back and told her yes, and that Jon and I were looking after you.'

'Oh. I'm so sorry Kate, you're a star...'

'No problem. Are you alone?'

Poppy forced herself to smile, hoping it might sound in her voice. 'No. I've got Belle with me.'

'Not what I meant, Poppy. I'm coming round.'

'No... Look, I'm really sorry. Dylan was here when I went into labour and things all happened so quickly that I didn't get a chance to call anyone. And then I didn't phone you because I knew you'd come and...' Poppy felt a tear run down her face, and thanked goodness this wasn't a video call. 'I just wanted you and Jon to have a romantic Christmas together. Hanging around in the hospital isn't much of a break when you work there.'

'Poppy! One of the things that Jon and I like about each other is that we're both part of a caring profession. What's he going to think if I leave my good friend and her day-old baby on her own on Christmas Day?'

Dylan had left her alone, but then Poppy had made it very clear that she didn't want him here. And he'd always listened to what she wanted.

'You don't have to tell Jon. Just get the rose petals out...'

'Too late. He's got his coat on, so it looks as if he's coming too. Hang on…' Kate called to Jon, 'Don't forget the food, sweetheart.'

'You're bringing food?' It sounded as if Kate was serious about this.

'Were you cooking this morning?'

'Kate, it's really kind of you. But I really just want to sleep…'

'You can sleep. Jon can stare lovingly at me holding the baby and make some turkey and cranberry sandwiches.'

Poppy sighed. Actually, turkey and cranberry sandwiches sounded really nice. She was hungry and maybe food and a little company would take her mind off wanting to cry all the time. 'If you're sure… Hold on.' Belle had started to cry and Poppy switched her phone to loudspeaker and picked her daughter up.

'Ooh. I heard her—she sounds so cute. I've *got* to come now…'

Poppy gave in to the inevitable. 'Okay. I'd love to see you both.'

'We'll be there in an hour. Send a photograph, so I can look at it in the car…'

Tidying away the wrapping paper that still lay on the coffee table and returning her wedding photo to its place on the sideboard had made Poppy feel a little better. When she looked at the plant next to it, she saw that the cracked pot had been repaired and there was no evidence of broken glass anywhere. *She* should have been the one to do all this, but Dylan's gesture had shown respect, for her and for Nate. More than that, it had shown a kindness that had been willing to understand her needs.

The thought only made her cry again. But it wasn't all about Poppy's needs. Dylan had given up a lot to support her and she was grateful, but he had his own life to live. Poppy couldn't give him what he deserved and she had to set him free.

Kate and Jon's arrival did take her mind off things a little. They plied Poppy with food, made a fuss of Belle and sat beside Poppy on the sofa for her video call to Germany, convincing her mum that they were all having a great Christmas.

'You guys, I just can't thank you enough.'

'What? Is that a hint, Poppy?' Kate looked at her watch. 'It's not even six o'clock. We're not going yet, are we, Jon?'

Jon chuckled. 'No, we're not.' He rose from his chair, collecting up the plates and glasses, ignoring Poppy when she told him that she could do it.

'You two are both as stubborn as each other.' She put her arm around Kate.

Kate chuckled. 'Yeah. How's your Christmas been so far?'

'Unlike any Christmas I've ever had before.'

'I can imagine. I assume that the *"friend from the hospital"* that your mum was talking about was Dylan?'

Poppy nodded. 'Yes. I was waiting to talk to Mum and Dad about that when they get home.'

'Yeah, good thought. That kind of thing's better in person.' Kate thought for a moment. 'Did Dylan leave you on your own this morning?'

'I know you don't like him...'

Kate held her hands up. 'That's not true! He's very dedicated and he's a really nice guy as well. And I freely admit that I was mistaken over Jeannie, and I'm really sorry that I ever mentioned it to you. But the thing is that we both believed it, didn't we? He's a player, and everyone knows it.'

'He has his reasons.' That sounded as if Poppy was defending him. Maybe she was.

'I'm sure he does. We all have our reasons. But however nice he is, however good-looking, you're the one who's my friend. That's the way it works.'

'I made him go, Kate. Because of *my* reasons.'

'Nate?'

Poppy nodded.

Still in love with Nate. That had once been so easy, so understandable. But it had all become more complicated in the last few weeks. She'd lost Nate and now she was afraid of losing Dylan.

She wasn't sure she could explain it to herself, let alone anyone else.

Kate hugged her tightly. 'You have Belle to think about now, honey.'

Belle shifted in her crib, opening her eyes, as if she knew that someone was talking about her. Poppy picked her up, holding the tiny baby in her arms. Just feeling her close seemed to turn on all the right hormones, and it was difficult not to smile. Belle was wide awake now, those blue eyes of hers tugging at Poppy's heart.

'Hello there, darling. You want to see your Auntie Kate?'

Kate grinned, stretching out her arms. 'Yes, she does! I definitely saw her perk up when you said my name. Come here, sweetie.'

Poppy's mum and dad had left their car in Germany and flown back home, arriving straight from Heathrow. Poppy had tidied the flat, and her mother had cooed over Belle for a while before plunging into the kitchen.

'She's not going to find all that much to do. Kate and Jon got there first—Jon even cleaned the oven.'

She'd given Belle to her dad to hold and he was taking the job seriously, rocking the tiny baby and talking to her. It was a moment before he replied.

'She'll find something. Any plumbing problems? Your mother's a dab hand with a wrench.'

Poppy laughed. It felt strange, when all she'd been doing lately was trying not to cry.

'Since when?'

'Since October. She and her friend have been going to evening classes on home management, and I got home one day to find that she'd mended a leak under the kitchen sink.'

'Good for her. I'll bear that in mind.'

'And what about you?' Her father's attention was suddenly all on Poppy.

'The midwife says that Belle's doing beautifully, she's feeding well and she only really cries when she's hungry.'

Her dad nodded. 'I was asking about *you*.'

Poppy had been trying to avoid that question. 'I'd be lying if I said I wasn't a bit tired, but it was an uncomplicated birth, and I'm getting along fine. The midwife says I'm doing beautifully, too.'

'Not singing the blues, then?'

That was what her dad had said to her when she was little, whenever she was upset about something. He always seemed to know, better than anyone, and he knew now.

'It's hormones, Dad. You remember when Mum had us?'

Her dad chuckled. 'Vividly. Belle's a lot more

serene than you were—you were so alert, and it was difficult to get you to sleep at times. She's more like your sisters.'

Or maybe more like Dylan. He was determined and forward-looking at work, but he had a quietness about him at times, the ability to just switch off and relax, that few people at the hospital ever saw. A rock-steady solidity that she'd allowed herself to depend on, even before she'd noticed it.

Don't cry. Dad'll notice, even if no one else does...

'Nate?' Her dad said the name quietly.

'Nate's gone, Dad. It was hard, but this is me moving on now.'

She *was* moving on. She'd always love Nate, but Poppy could say his name without wanting to break down and sob. She could see in his face that her dad didn't quite believe her, but he wasn't going to be satisfied with *It's complicated...*

'I hear you've had plenty of help from your friends while we've been away. Your mother's furious…'

Had they heard something?

'What about?'

'She wanted to be here for you. I've never seen anyone vent so much anger at snow before.'

'Bloody snow!' Mum's voice drifted in unexpectedly from the kitchen, and Poppy laughed with her dad.

'It's good to have you here now,' Poppy called through to her mother.

It was *really* good, better than either of them knew. Belle had seen her tears, even if Poppy had instinctively tried to hide them, and she must be glad her grandparents were here too.

'It's all been fine.' Poppy turned to her dad, smiling and lowering her voice, just in case her mum felt undervalued. 'A friend had popped round to see me on Christmas Eve, and took me straight to the hospital when I went into labour. Then stayed with me during the birth.'

Poppy carefully avoided the use of pronouns, in case her dad picked up on the idea that there was a male friend involved. That would have to come later, when she could tell them about Dylan without betraying her feelings.

'And it was *snowing*…' Poppy grinned at her dad conspiratorially. 'I could hear the Christmas bells in the distance…'

'I was wondering where you got the name from.' Her dad grinned down at Belle, mouthing her name. 'She's a real Christmas Belle, with those blue eyes.'

'They may darken…' Poppy was becoming more and more sure that they wouldn't. Maybe that was just wishful thinking. Something of

Dylan's that she could keep for ever. He'd texted every day to ask how she and Belle were, and Poppy had replied, sending new pictures of Belle. Just Belle. There was a void between her and Dylan now that seemed impossible to cross.

'Hey, now…' Her dad had had more practice at baby-juggling than Poppy, and managed to reach over and put his arm around her while keeping Belle cradled safe and secure in his other arm. Poppy realised that a tear had escaped custody and was making a run for it, down her cheek.

'It's nothing, Dad. Hormones will be hor-mones.'

'I know. That's the trouble with you doctors.'

'What? We have more hormones than every-one else? I'm not aware of *that* condition.'

Her dad chuckled. 'No. You think everything's a chemical reaction. Hasn't this little girl taught you one thing, darling? Some things are all about the heart.'

CHAPTER FOURTEEN

I⊤ WAS ALMOST New Year. Poppy had two New Year's resolutions, the first of which was to get through the day. The second was a little more challenging, because it was to get through the night.

She'd thought the tears might pass, but as she and Belle had started to get into a routine, and Poppy began to feel stronger and more confident, they'd only become more frequent. More focused on Dylan and the agreement they'd made.

He'd asked her if there was anything she needed, pretty much every time he texted. And there *was* something that Poppy needed. He was off work on New Year's Eve and Poppy suggested that he might like to video call, so he could see Belle. His reply had been an enthusiastic *yes* and he'd said he'd be ready any time they were.

Poppy was ready.

She fed Belle and bundled her up in as many layers of clothing as she could. Then took a few layers off again, in case she overheated. A pair of trousers and a zipped sweater that she hadn't been able to fit into for months, but which were now both satisfyingly loose-fitting, would have to do for her, and running a comb through her hair. Because the taxi she'd booked would be here soon. Poppy fixed the baby carrier into the pram attachment, whispering to Belle that now was the time to be on her very best behaviour, and made her way downstairs to wait for the taxi in the lobby.

Dylan almost didn't answer when his intercom sounded. He'd been sitting in front of his tablet, waiting. Poppy had said ten o'clock, and he'd already cleaned and tidied his whole flat, more as a matter of calming his nerves than anything. Practically speaking, just the background of where he was sitting would have done, but then he'd already changed his mind about that several times, and was thinking about doing so again.

The intercom, again. If it was a parcel then they could leave it at the door, and anyone who'd just decided to pop in unannounced would find him unavailable for visitors. But it sounded a third time, and Dylan strode impatiently over to the console.

'What?' Maybe that wasn't a particularly genial greeting for a courier who was just doing their job. 'Would you leave it at the door, please?'

'Leave what at the door? Me or Belle?'

Dylan's heart almost jumped out of his chest when he heard Poppy's voice. He automatically pressed the downstairs door release, and then realised he should say something.

'Poppy? Poppy...'

'I'm coming up. See you in a minute.'

He heard the sound of the door slamming behind her and realised he'd forgotten to ask her if she was all right. Dylan hurried out into the lift lobby, staring at the lights on the two floor indicators.

Think.

Calling the lift and going downstairs to meet her might well leave him in the main lobby and Poppy up here. If something was wrong, then the quickest way of finding out was to stay put. One of the lift cars was travelling steadily upwards, and he positioned himself by the doors.

Poppy was smiling. That was all he saw for a moment, and it told him everything he needed to know. She looked a little nervous, but there was no emergency. All the same, Dylan asked.

'You're okay? And Belle?'

'Yes. I thought you might like to hold her. And I want to talk...'

'Yes.' There was only one word to say in response to all of that. Talking sounded a little ominous, but not talking had been the hardest thing he'd ever done. Dylan stood back, catching the lift door before it started to close. Everything he wanted, everything he'd ever need, was here right now and he wouldn't waste a moment of it. He'd trusted her and he'd waited. And Poppy had come. Now was the time to put up a fight.

When he ushered her through his front door he wished he'd left the Christmas decorations up for a little longer. But they'd seemed to mock his unhappiness, and he'd called the company who'd put them up and asked them to come and take them down again. They'd left the flat spotless, but feeling cold and unloved. Which had been okay, because it had matched his mood exactly.

Perhaps if he switched on a few lights... But there was no time for that because Poppy was pulling down the hood of the baby carrier, and loosening some of the baby blankets that she'd wrapped around her daughter. Dylan caught his breath.

'She's even more beautiful than I remember.'

Poppy nodded. 'I feel that every morning when I get up.'

Dylan was about to ask if he might hold her and then remembered, running his fingers ruefully across his chin. A five o'clock shadow had been fine for video conferencing, but he didn't want Belle's fingers to reach for him and find stubble. 'I…didn't shave.'

Poppy looked up at him solemnly. Something was up and he could feel cold dread clutching at his heart. Maybe she'd come to a decision that would part them for good. He ran through the options. Meeting someone was unlikely in the circumstances… Emigrating…? More likely, but distance wouldn't get in his way. He'd meet whatever happened next and deal with it.

'Seems that she loves the movement of a car, and she's sleeping now. Could we talk first?'

'Yes, of course.'

Poppy hadn't taken her coat off yet and that was a worry. Then he remembered that Belle was her first priority, and that Poppy had removed all but one of the blankets that were wrapped around her. He waved her over to the seating area, and waited for Poppy to choose where she sat.

'Keep an eye on her…' She parked the baby carrier in front of one of the sofas and pointed to the seat right next to it, indicating that he should sit down. Then she moved to the opposite sofa. Face to face, but too far away.

Dylan turned his gaze to Belle. The love was different, but it was difficult to say which was more overwhelming. He couldn't think about that now. He had to listen to whatever it was that Poppy needed to say, and just take each moment as it came.

Dylan seemed tired. Shocked to see her, and then as nervous as Poppy felt. Maybe she should have given him some warning of this, but he'd asked what she needed. And she needed this. Just this one chance to say what was on her mind, and then he could shut her out if he wanted to.

She took a breath. She'd rehearsed this a thousand times, but she was going to have to wing it, because everything was different now. Just seeing him seemed to change everything.

'We didn't choose this, Dylan. I thought that the way I felt about you was all about the baby, and that I couldn't love anyone after Nate died. But I was wrong.'

She saw him catch his breath. Maybe… But Poppy couldn't even think it, that hope hurt too badly.

'Nate will always have a piece of my heart. I thought that Belle would fill the rest of it, and she has. But somehow there's more. That doesn't follow any of the physiological rules…' She shrugged and Dylan smiled.

'Yeah. I understand.'

He was waiting for her to finish. Waiting to

hear what she had to say. Right now, she needed his help.

'Poppy. Please just say it, whatever it is. I know you'll always want the best for Belle and so do I.' There was warmth in his eyes now, and Poppy could feel that some of it was for her.

She took a breath. 'Dylan, you'll always be Belle's father, and there are no conditions on you seeing her, we don't come as a package. But I want you to know that the part of my heart that belongs to today is all yours.'

Suddenly everything was for her. The look in his beautiful eyes, the way that he smiled. Poppy felt heat rising to her cheeks, and realised that some of it was because she still had her coat on. She loosened the buttons and Dylan got to his feet, walking around the coffee table. Her legs almost gave way as she got to her feet and as he helped her out of her coat she realised he was shaking too.

'Belle...' She looked across at the baby carrier, not daring to meet Dylan's gaze.

'She's fast asleep. This is between you and me, Poppy.' Dylan took her hand and she wound her fingers around his, holding on to him.

'You know...you're my worst nightmare...'

Poppy knew what that meant, and returned his smile. 'I'm going to take that as a compliment.'

'You should. I used to dread getting involved

226 NEUROSURGEON'S IVF MIX-UP MIRACLE

with anyone, feeling any of the feelings that went with that. But I couldn't help falling in love with you, Poppy. And I couldn't fight any more. I knew I had to wait and let you come back to me.'

She felt tears form in her eyes. 'You did that for me, Dylan? You're the best and nicest man I know...'

'I did it for both of us. You've been through so much in the last month, but I knew you had the strength to follow your heart, and I just had to find it in my heart to trust you.'

'I'm sorry...'

He laid his finger on her lips. 'Don't you dare apologise. The first promise I made to you was that nothing happens before you're ready, and I'm sticking by it.'

'I'm ready, Dylan. I couldn't bear the idea of losing you, the way I lost Nate, and so I sold you both short, by burying myself in my memories. But I've made my decision and I'm here now.'

'We need a new set of promises.'

'Looks like it...' Poppy wasn't afraid any more. Dylan knew her, better than anyone else, and the tenderness in his face told her that he wouldn't hurt her.

'Poppy Evans. Will you be my worst nightmare? For the rest of my life.'

'That's...a very long time.' If she could believe

in Dylan, then she could bring herself to trust that it *would* be a very long time.

He smiled. 'Yes, it is. It may be scary because nightmares often are, and there's a lot we both need to come to terms with. But I promise you that I'll always love you.'

'I'll be your nightmare, if you'll be mine.'

He wound his arms around her shoulders, letting out a sigh. She could feel his body against hers, hear his heart pounding and feel the tremble of his limbs, but that was subsiding now. Warmth began to curl around them, in an exquisite reminder that the here and now were everything. Dylan was everything, even if that flouted the laws of mathematics, because Belle was everything too.

'I'm putting you on notice.' He seemed to have abandoned his usual habit of giving Poppy the options and letting her make up her mind. 'We might stumble a bit, and neither of us knows what the future's going to be like. But I won't leave you. We'll wake up together and face the day together. Every day.'

'That's what I want, Dylan. Because I'll always love you.'

Poppy could feel sweet arousal begin to throb in her veins. She wasn't ready for that, and she wasn't entirely sure that she wanted Dylan to see her body right now. But this was stronger. She kissed him, holding him tight, and his response made her knees tremble. Tender and yet full of that sweet passion that seemed to drive him forward in everything he did.

'Dylan...'

'No.' He held her in his arms and she could feel he wanted exactly the same as her. Even if she was a little afraid. 'Absolutely not, Poppy.'

'Maybe we could... I don't know...'

'Exactly. We'll wait until you *do* know. We have time.'

The thought of time, stretching out before them and beckoning them on, made her smile. 'You're probably right.'

He grinned. 'For the avoidance of doubt... I have the most beautiful woman in my arms and I want to make love to you, right now. The one thing I want more is to wait until you know you're ready. We don't have to prove anything to each other, do we?'

'No, we don't.' Poppy smiled up at him. 'I rather like this new you. The one who tells me exactly what *he* wants.'

He chuckled. 'I'm relying on you to tell me exactly what you want back.'

Poppy could do that. When Dylan's demanding side came to the fore, it was all about how they could move forward together. Not about him at all, but about the best for both of them.

She heard Belle shift, and her head turned instinctively. Dylan's had too. Belle's thin cry sounded and he let her go, making the action seem both urgent and still a little reluctant.

'Our daughter has exquisite timing.'

'Tell me that at two in the morning.' Poppy poked him gently in the ribs. 'Aren't you going to do something about her exquisite timing, then? Since you're her dad.'

Dylan chuckled in delight, moving over to the baby carrier and gently lifting Belle into his arms, making sure she couldn't reach the stubble on his chin. There it was. There had been a thousand pictures of Belle but Poppy didn't need a camera for this one. The image would always be burned into her memory. The man she loved, gently quieting their daughter.

Poppy had sat down to feed Belle and, after a moment's hesitation and her smiling nod, Dylan had taken his place next to her on the sofa, his arm around her. Feeding Belle always gave Poppy a feeling of well-being, but right now her endorphin levels must be going through the roof. Belle wasn't ready to go back to sleep yet, sensing maybe that today was special. Poppy was happy, and the two people she loved most in the world were happy too.

'You want to come back to mine?'

He hesitated. Poppy knew it was nothing to do with her or Belle, and had everything to do with bricks and mortar.

'I've made my peace with Nathan. I'll always love him, but he's gone. It's time to make new memories, and you, me and Belle belong together now.' She grinned up at him. 'Along with a small mountain of baby paraphernalia.'

'Sounds good to me.' He kissed her, and Poppy knew that everything was going to be all right.

'I'll get Belle ready to go, then?'

'In a minute. I've got something for you. A present for you when you had the baby.'

'Dylan, that's so sweet. Can I open it now?'

He chuckled at her excitement. 'Of course. Then we'll go over to yours, eh?'

They lay together on the bed, both propped up on pillows. Belle was sleeping in her crib and Poppy and Dylan were stargazing.

'I love this so much, Dylan.' Poppy snuggled against him, feeling his warmth. 'It's such a beautiful present, stars all the way across the ceiling. And they're so bright and clear.'

He'd made her stay in the sitting room with Belle while he fiddled with the star projector, setting it up and getting the focus right. And when he'd finally called her into the bedroom it had seemed like a whole new world, just waiting for her. He'd changed into sweatpants and a T-shirt, and Poppy had put on a cotton nightdress with a warm dressing gown, ready for their first night together. It was already more than she could have dreamed it might be.

Dylan kissed her forehead. Kissing was underrated and they'd been exploring every aspect of kissing under the stars.

Belle woke a little before it was time for her feed and Poppy picked her up, hushing her. 'Take your T-shirt off.'

'You want to look without touching?' he joked, and Poppy chuckled.

'Yeah, I do. That's not why I asked. It's time you two did a little bonding.'

Poppy allowed herself a smile as he pulled his T-shirt over his head, and then she took off Belle's sleepsuit and laid her down on his chest. She quietened immediately and Dylan's goofy smile surfaced as Poppy laid a baby blanket over Belle's tiny body.

'She's so warm. This feels…'

'Like nothing else?'

'Yeah.' He cradled Belle gently, and Poppy moved to get back onto the bed. This was what he must have felt when Belle was born, a craving to be close to both of them.

Dylan let out a sigh of pure contentment. 'What did I do to deserve this?'

'You promised me the stars, Dylan. Seems you've just delivered...'

EPILOGUE

Three years later

Six o'clock in the morning. Poppy opened her eyes to the sound of Belle singing in the room next door. She nudged Dylan, watching as his eyes opened. She never tired of that.

'It's worked. She hasn't got all the words yet, but the tune's almost perfect.' Dylan had been singing 'Chapel of Love' to Belle for weeks now. 'Just in time, as well.'

Dylan chuckled. 'Seems we've done a few things just in time lately.'

They'd started off with everything the wrong way round. Had a baby, and then made love. That first, tender night had been so special, but then Dylan had shown her how perfect could be improved upon. He'd understood why Poppy felt anxious about marriage, and that it was all about her fear of losing him rather than any reluctance to commit herself. But as soon as Poppy was happy with the idea they'd started to look for a venue, finding that it was easier than they'd expected to book exactly what they wanted for a mid-December wedding.

It had been a short and very sweet engagement, made even sweeter when they'd found that Poppy was pregnant again, just last week. Dylan had said that telling everyone after they returned from their honeymoon would be soon enough, and Poppy had joked that they were finally doing things in the right order.

And now Belle was singing just the right song, on just the right day. Dylan kissed her, getting out of bed and pulling on a pair of jeans and a sweater. But Belle's love of moving forward rivalled even his, and she burst into their room.

'Dad... Dad!'

'What is it?' Dylan caught Belle in his arms, swinging her around, then set her back onto her feet, squatting on his heels in front of her.

'Are we all getting married today?'

Dylan chuckled. 'Yep. I suppose we are—because we can't do it without you. You know what happens before that, Belle?'

Belle knew. Dylan was so good with her, encouraging her to be a little less impatient without quashing her natural exuberance and her desire to move forward, which reminded Poppy so much of him.

'Stop. And. Think...' Belle snuggled against

him. Two pairs of beautiful blue eyes and two blonde heads, Belle's hair a little lighter and finer than Dylan's.

'Yeah, that's right. We're getting married this afternoon, so what will we do this morning?' Dylan started to count on his fingers. 'We could sit quietly and watch Mummy curl her hair...'

'No!' Belle laughed up at him.

'Right, then. Go to the playground in the park?'

Belle looked at him, undecided. She liked the park, but she knew as well as Poppy did that Dylan always saved the best for last.

'Okay, that's a maybe. Or we could go to the hospital where Mummy and Daddy work and see the Christmas lights in the garden.'

'Yes!'

'Right, then. We'll need to get dressed first. One...two...three...'

'Go!' Belle shouted, running from the room, and Dylan walked back to the bed, kissing Poppy.

'You are *such* a nice man, Mr Harper. That's going to take you almost three hours.' They'd moved away from central London, and the cash from both of their flats had allowed them to buy a house with a large garden.

'Say three and a half, if we stop for breakfast. That gives you time for a lie-in, and then you can go over to your parents' place. Kate'll be there to help you with your dress, and Sophie's bringing Thomas over at eleven. I'll drop Belle over on the way back, and Sophie can help wrangle her into her dress, while I come home and get into my suit.'

'And then we're…'

He grinned, climbing back onto the bed to kiss her. 'Nearly forgot. We're getting married.' Dylan's hand found its way under the covers, caressing her stomach. 'What do you reckon. Boy or girl?'

'Now who's racing ahead? We'll get married, and go on our honeymoon…'

'Northern Lights, reindeer and lots of snow. And Father Christmas, of course…' Dylan grinned boyishly. 'Very long nights at this time of year.'

'So that's something for all three of us. Then we'll come home, take a breath, and find out in due course whether it's a boy or a girl.'

'Good thought.' Dylan kissed her again, climbing off the bed. 'See you later, sweetheart.'

The bedroom door closed behind him, and Poppy smiled, wide awake now but luxuriating in the warm pleasure of not having to get up just yet.

The doors ahead of the bridal party swung open. As soon as Poppy and Dylan had seen this place they'd known that it was where they wanted to be married. One of the oldest banqueting halls in London, it had been recently restored into a high arched space for weddings, which satisfied even Dylan's sense of the dramatic.

Poppy had insisted on a child-friendly ceremony, and her older nieces and nephews were all part of the bridal procession. Sam was at the front, juggling his best man duties with his two-year-old daughter, who would have a good view of the ceremony from her father's arms. Kate was in charge of the other bridesmaids and pageboys, and was chivvying them into their places so that at least they'd start off in a straight line, even if they didn't finish that way.

'Ready?' Her father nudged her, and she nodded. Poppy couldn't take her eyes off Dylan, who was waiting with Sam at the head of the aisle. So handsome in his dark blue suit, the flowers in his buttonhole matching the ones she was carrying. He'd loved her so faithfully and truly, and she couldn't wait to marry him.

'I'm ready.'

Kate let go of Belle's hand, stepping back to walk with the other bridesmaids. Belle raced down the aisle, scattering petals in all directions, while Thomas followed at a more sedate pace with the rings. Poppy's dad guided her forward, blind to everything other than the man she was about to marry. She was dimly aware that

Sam had caught Belle's hand, showing her and Thomas where to stand, and then her dad ushered her to Dylan's side.

'You look beautiful.' He murmured the words, taking her hand, and Poppy smiled up at him.

Suddenly the world shot back into sharp focus as the celebrant stepped forward, welcoming everyone.

The words they'd helped write seemed even more beautiful in this setting. So much more binding when spoken aloud in front of their families and friends. When Poppy promised to love Dylan always she saw a tear form in his eye, and she paused for a moment to wipe it away. And when the ceremony was concluded, and Dylan kissed her, it felt as if he was doing so for the very first time.

'How did we do?' Poppy looked up at him. Their walk together, back down the aisle, had been delayed for a few minutes as Belle and the other children crowded around them excitedly.

'I think we did just fine.' Dylan's face was shining with happiness. 'Now it's just the rest of our lives…'

'Piece of cake.' Poppy grinned at him and he chuckled.

'Yeah. My thoughts entirely.'

* * * * *